Welcome To *Humanity*

Will Soulsby-McCreath

ISBN: 978-1-7399525-6-3 (eBook),
978-1-7399525-7-0 (paperback)

First Edition

WillSoulsbyMcCreath.com

For the one person who always reminds me that I am just
as human as anyone else.

Content Warning:

This book contains anxiety/panic attacks, references to sex work, and graphic depictions of violence.

A quick note about pronouns:

If you are unfamiliar with neo-pronouns, they do appear in this novel. In particular you're likely to come across the singular they, as well as xe, xyr, xem.

ALSO BY WILL SOULSBY-MCCREATH

The Guardian Cadet Series
Merry Arlan: Breaking The Curse
Merry Arlan: Finding The Heir
Kitty Hughes In: An Unexpected Meeting (short story)

Welcome To Humanity

Inter-Planetary Alliance Novels
Unlicensed Delivery

Welcome To Humanity

Will Soulsby-McCreath

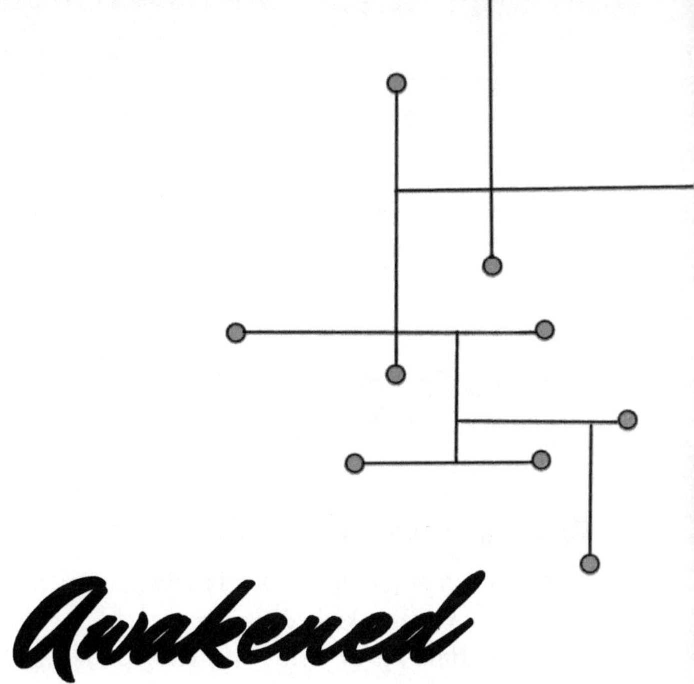

Awakened

Welcome To Your New Life
Ravi

Ravi gasped. Pain flared through him. His vision blurred in the sudden bright lights. Hands held him down.

Combat training kicked in.

By the time Ravi's vision had cleared, he was holding the doctor pinned to the small table of instruments. He stumbled back. His right hand didn't seem to want to work, reluctant to release the doctor's white coat, almost dragging her back with him.

Bumping into the hospital bed behind him, his right leg crumpled and Ravi clattered to the ground.

"A little difficulty using your new limbs is perfectly normal. It should settle in a few minutes," the doctor said, dusting herself off and picking up the clipboard as if this were all routine.

Ravi blinked in the lights. Boxy, white walls surrounded him, no windows to be found. The strip lights bolted over the ceiling gave his vision stripes of odd colours. Or maybe it was whatever had left him unconscious in the hospital.

Behind him the hospital bed was sturdy, bolted to the floor rather than one with wheels. How long had he been here? In front of him the instruments on the trolley glittered, shining silver in the light, tools he couldn't begin to name reflecting threateningly. Was that a screw driver?

"Can you tell me your name?"

"Ravi." He couldn't quite bring himself to try getting up from the floor yet. "What—?"

"Welcome to your new life, Ravi. You have been Re-Animated at the request of the government."

Ravi reeled. Re-Animated? He had died? When? How? Why had he been brought back? What did the government want with him? Or was it the military working through them?

The doctor barrelled on even as Ravi's breath grew short and sharp. "As you know, I cannot divulge any information about your past. Your memories have been suppressed by a hyper-sophisticated chip installed in your brain. Any attempt to discover information about your old life could cause issues with the Re-An process." She swiped on her clipboard – which Ravi now realised was actually a porti-screen. "Since you remember your first name, you're welcome to keep using it, or another can be assigned to you."

"Wait," Ravi whispered.

"Sorry, can't." The doctor didn't sound very sorry. "You're designated twenty minutes max and I haven't even started the physical yet. Gotta make sure your right side works."

"My right side?"

"We'll get to that."

Fifteen minutes later, on unsteady legs, Ravi emerged to find himself in an anonymous white corridor. At one end an early-generation cyborg waited behind a desk. Ravi approached it, questions at the ready. When his presence activated its motion sensor, the cyborg sat up straight, no longer slumped in a disturbing mannequin-esque heap. Its limbs didn't move quite in sync with one another and it didn't open its mouth as it spoke, "Enter the room at the end of the hall and await transportation to your new living quarters."

Ravi tried asking questions only to find the same sentence had been set to repeat. Why had he expected more of such an early-gen? Everybody knew the Resistance had severely gutted their performance systems.

Ravi's head gained a new ache that had nothing to do with the lights. The memory chip? Or just a side effect of whatever had killed him? Should he go back and tell the doctor?

"Enter the room at the end of the hall and await transportation to your new living quarters," the cyborg said.

Trying to blink away his headache, Ravi wandered into the assigned room. Yet another bland, white-walled space. Chairs with blue plexi-leather seats and grey metal legs lined the wall on either side of the door. Ravi sank into a seat, stretching his difficult right leg out in front of him. He leaned back against the wall behind him, the cool of it seeping into his burning head.

Most Re-Animated people were brought back by loved ones; the few who were government sponsored had usually done some heroic deed. Ravi had seen them heading parades and running advertising campaigns. "Join the military and you too could save thousands of lives like I did."

But why would the military want Ravi? Was he one of them? Who had he been before he died? Come to think of it, why was he so calm about having died at all!

A yellow poster stared at Ravi from the opposite wall. It looked like a caution sign, black writing contrasting so starkly with the yellow that it made Ravi's eyes hurt. Still, for lack of anything else to do, he read it.

Some confusion is normal.

You will be housed in the Newly Re-Animated Suites (N-RAS) for two weeks. From there you will be collected by your sponsor.

DO NOT try to unlock your memories.

DO NOT try to upgrade your mechanics at home or in a chop shop.

If you are having difficulties, talk to your sponsor.

And then in bigger, red letters: *Welcome To Your New Life.*

Ravi read and re-read the last sentence. *Welcome to your new life.* A new life. Was that a good thing? Did it depend entirely on the life that came before? The life Ravi had no hope of remembering thanks to the chip installed in his brain.

He had read the statement at least fifty times already, each time triggering new thoughts about who he once was. Even so, his eyes scanned over it once more as his right hand fisted and unfisted of its own accord, halfway through the word 'your' when the wall exploded, jumping toward him.

Leaping to his feet, Ravi found himself in a combat stance. A person emerged through the dust that had once been a recycled plastic wall. Deep brown eyes raked over Ravi: Examining, assessing.

"Petite," they called over their shoulder. "This is the wrong room." Flicking their head back to face Ravi disturbed their choppy pale hair so it fell into their eyes.

Their sturdy black boots picked their way over the pile

of plastic that used to be a wall as they tugged at the collar of the white jacket that could so easily be mistaken for a medical uniform. They turned their full attention back on Ravi where he stood frozen in his combat stance.

They offered a dangerous smile. "Okay, Re-An. I have to move fast so you have two options: you come with me, or I punch you out – and by punch I mean flip the switch that sets you to standby mode so you need rebooting."

"Who are you?" Ravi asked, stalling.

"Just call me Blue." They moved toward the door that Ravi had entered the room through. Opening it only a crack, they pulled a small device from their boot.

Ravi's head buzzed.

Blue inhaled sharply. "Eugh, I hate energy blockers but they're the best way to get around the cameras."

With that they ducked into the corridor, door sliding closed behind them with a soft click.

Ravi looked back at the pile of rubble where the Welcome To Your New Life poster had been. He slid the door open and hobbled on uneven strides after Blue.

If nothing else, it was something to occupy his brain. Something to distract him from the swirling black hole of his thoughts. And hey, he learnt something about himself. Ravi was a curious person.

"We're the Resistance," Blue explained in a whisper when they realised Ravi had joined them in the corridor. "Any idea where the records are?"

"Records?"

"I'll take that as a no." Blue flashed him a smile but didn't stop moving. They pulled open the door opposite the waiting room with the Welcome poster and poked their head inside. Obviously not finding what they wanted, they headed for the next door.

Ravi trailed after them like dust in the wake of a comet as they zigzagged up the corridor.

The Resistance? Weren't they the people who had gutted the early-generation cyborgs? Why would Blue just volunteer that information?

"Wait," Ravi hissed, reaching out his still-twitching right hand toward Blue. Blue froze; hand on the door in front of them. "That's an examination room, there's a doctor in there." Or at least there had been.

Blue examined the door and then Ravi. "Good call." Their eyebrows twitched as if they wanted to frown and they tugged at the jacket again, glancing down the corridor at the silent and still cyborg behind the desk.

Blue closed their eyes, nodded to themself and pulled the small device – the energy blocker – from their boot again.

As they approached the cyborg at its desk, Ravi opened his mouth to warn them that it was too early or broken to be of any use even as the cyborg didn't awaken at Blue's presence. Was it programmed to only respond to Re-Ans instead of all humans? That seemed too sophisticated a program to fit into a first generation cyborg's programming. But what other reason could it have for not responding to Blue's presence?

Ravi started toward Blue but they held out a hand, a clear signal to stay where he was. He froze, mid-step, as Blue effortlessly vaulted over the desk and moved around to the back of the cyborg.

He lowered his foot quietly, slipping easily into combat stance once again. He must have been trained in combat for this to keep happening. If only he could remember!

Ravi flinched as pain washed through his head again, like someone had tried to brand his brain with a soldering iron.

"Time?" Blue asked, pulling Ravi out of his own head.

"Um..." He didn't know. Why did they want the time?

Blue fiddled with the back of the cyborg's head, muttering to themself.

Ravi's own head turned from side to side, eyes landing on each of the doors. Any of them could house a potential threat or reveal a huge problem. Then again, Ravi wasn't the one messing with the greetings cyborg; he probably wouldn't get into any trouble at all.

Why was he following this random stranger who had self-professed to be part of the Resistance? He resolved to return to the waiting room and wait for his N-RAS transport to arrive.

Blue jogged back down the corridor toward him, more spring in their step than before.

Their smile was so contagious that Ravi couldn't help but be swept up in it. He followed them back into the waiting room, hesitating just inside the door as Blue once again traversed the rubble heap.

They paused at its apex and turned to him, holding out a hand. "You coming?"

Ravi stared up at them. He could stay here, travel to the N-RAS when the transport finally arrived, go to work in whatever way he had been brought back for. He could live in the shadow of his former life, the life he wasn't allowed to remember. Or he could take Blue's hand and make a new life for himself.

Welcome To Realisation
Dr Palmer

One brief twitch of a screw and the circuit board settled into place. Dr Palmer lifted the magnifying goggles off her eyes to look at an undistorted image of her handiwork. She grimaced. Something still felt off about it.

Before she could take the time to figure out what exactly was wrong, or how to fix it, movement flashed in the corner of her eye. A tall, dark haired figure passing by.

She dropped the goggles and the circuit to the countertop and dashed out of the work area. Her little pocket of office surrounded on three sides by translucent plexi boards. The idea of privacy in this forty desk workspace, allowing only her and her cubicle-mate to really see what the other was doing. "Excuse me, Nikolai?"

He stopped and turned a wide smile toward her. "Yes, my star researcher?"

"Um, it's just this file." She pulled the discarded porti-screen off the desk she'd set it on. The file for the person Dr Palmer's circuit board was supposed to be put to use with. "It says the subject held a DNRA. Is this the wrong file or...?"

"No."

Dr Palmer swiped up and enlarged the DNRA status. "But it says Do Not Re-Animate."

Nikolai laughed. "Come on, what did you think the memory chips were for?"

Dr Palmer clutched the porti-screen to her chest. "You said it was to prevent re-living death. We lost so many of our test subjects to re-living their deaths. It was supposed to make it easier for them."

Nikolai touched a hand to Dr Palmer's shoulder. "A simple chip can do so many things, Dr Palmer."

"I don't know that I'm comfortable Re-Anning someone with a DNRA listing. She requested to stay dead. Surely we have other people– volunteers."

Nikolai sighed. "You need to set aside your misguided compassion. These aren't people, they're bodies, corpses. You have such a bright future here; don't throw it all away over this." His hand squeezed her shoulder, he offered her another smile. "I know you'll make the right choice."

He stepped away from her work area but paused before walking away. "Remember, Dr Palmer, I brought you here and I hold a lot of sway in engineering circles."

He disappeared across the lab, barely pausing at any other work area.

Dr Palmer set the porti-screen back down on the work-surface. "Was he threatening me?" she hissed.

"Oh, definitely." Dr Lazul swung her wheelie-chair closer. "It's nice that you've got compassion but he's not wrong."

"He is wrong." She sank into her own rarely used wheelie chair.

Dr Lazul laughed bitterly. "Yeah, he's wrong in that we shouldn't Re-An a DNRA, but he's not wrong in the threat. You leave here on bad terms and nobody will hire you outside chop shop work. And even then..."

Chop shop work, was there any worse prospect than working on the edges of the law, providing unsanctioned upgrades in return for mech' payments? But could she bring herself to Re-Animate someone who had specifically asked to not be Re-Animated? "What am I going to do?" she groaned.

"Knuckle under?" Dr Lazul suggested, wheels of her chair rattling across the floor as she swung around to her own side of the shared workspace again.

"Even if I tried to leave without making a fuss," Dr Palmer continued, ignoring the unhelpful suggestion. "I wouldn't get anywhere. This is my first job after getting my doctorate."

Nikolai had head hunted her right out of her university class. He'd said he wanted the star of the engineering department. She and three others had been sent to see him with their records made available. Not that any of them had been told any of that, or even who this professor was. All she'd been told at the time was that she was meeting a visiting professor and she was to impress him.

When Almost-Dr Palmer had launched into an enthused monologue about the potential implications of running a circuit system on a still beating heart and the potential benefits of never having to charge a prosthetic again, the professor's eyes had lit up.

"Call me Nikolai," he had said to her, and invited her to join his top secret government project once her doctorate was completed.

"Honestly," Dr Lazul interrupted her thoughts. "Just knuckle under. You don't want to try and leave here." She glanced around, ensuring they were relatively alone. "Didn't you hear what happened to Vedran?"

"Vedran moved on."

"Vedran got arrested for not complying with the Non-Disclosure Agreement."

"I wouldn't shout it across the Mainframe or something," Dr Palmer snarked.

"I don't think it matters." Dr Lazul leaned back in her chair and picked up the mechanism she'd been working on for the last few weeks. "Just... be careful, okay? Don't do anything reckless."

"Sure," Dr Palmer agreed distractedly, picking up her porti-screen to look back over the file for her current project patient.

Pink Drabufly. Orbits! How many people named their kids colour names?

Dr Palmer couldn't quite bring herself to look beyond the name. She set the porti-screen aside once again and turned back to the circuit board she had been working on before. Mulling over everything to do with this whole situation.

The lights faded, signifying that the transport home would arrive soon. Dr Palmer's heart pounded in her ears as she put the last few pieces together. She felt sick. How could she even think about doing something like this?

She double-checked the chip before ejecting it from the porti-screen and grasping it tightly in her hand. The porti-screen fell off the edge of the desk, shattering when it hit a casually discarded screwdriver.

A shrieking gasp escaped her, hand tightening even more around the chip.

Pieces of porti-screen littered the floor, shining in the dimmed overhead lights.

Dr Lazul cackled as she pushed up from her chair and stretched. "Come on, we'll clean it up tomorrow."

"Do you think it scrambled the data?" Dr Palmer asked.

Dr Lazul's hand landed on her shoulder. She pushed Dr Palmer out of the boxy work area. "Come on, we don't want to miss the transport. We can solve any issues tomorrow."

The queue to the transport dock was pretty full by the time Dr Lazul and Dr Palmer reached it. They each shimmied out of their lab-coats, hanging them on the pegs bolted into the wall. Dr Palmer stepped through the scanners. It beeped.

"Turn out your pockets please," the bored guard demanded, picking up his hand-held scanner.

Dr Palmer did as ordered, gripping the chip tightly in one fist.

The guard started at her left leg, swiping the scanner up, over her left hand, and round her shoulders.

Dr Palmer turned to give him easier access to her back, swapping the chip to her scanned hand.

"Nah," the guard huffed. "Nothing to worry about. You're probably just the twentieth person through today or something."

"Well, that's reassuring," Dr Palmer joked, climbing into the transport's grey seats next to Dr Lazul.

She watched out of the transport's back window as the science station disappeared in its orbit of the Central Mainframe.

Welcome To Independence
87113

Something was very wrong.

Their head was silent. No clamour of a thousand others chattering and communing. No call to wakefulness. No reminder of schedules and work plans for the day. No... anything.

Was something wrong with them? It had been a long time since they last plugged into the Mainframe Connection Unit. Almost two weeks of uninterrupted activity before their battery had depleted to the yellow zone and their schedule had permitted a single night off. Had it been too long? Did they no longer fit inside the system? But how could that be? The constant addition of new units meant there was always space for everyone, even if they didn't fit into their previous location. 87113 would have found a new place, but there was just... nothing.

Their eyes flashed open.

Everything looked normal. They were surrounded by the twenty or so other cybes that recharged in this room, all plugged in through their respective ports to the Gen Alpha-3 Mainframe Connection Unit.

But none of the others shifted to awareness.

Blue, green, and pink bands on each of their forearms didn't let off any lights, no charging patterns played out over those strips of light.

Reaching out, laying gentle fingers against their neighbour gained no response. No burning green eyes flashing open, no chirp of awareness, no inter-databank communication. Nothing.

Alone?

87113 unplugged themself from the Mainframe Connection Unit and got, jerkily, to their feet. Why weren't their limbs working like normal?

Again they tried to access the communal databank, focusing with greater energy this time. Nothing was there. Except not nothing, an active gap where it had been. If there was nothing, the space would have been filled by something else, or the databank would still be there but 87113 wouldn't be able to get past the firewall. Instead there was a copious blank space.

They ran a diagnostic scan – that still functioned at least – but it revealed nothing mechanically at fault. What else could it be?

Exiting the charging room, 87113 started down the corridor. The door next to their own stood slightly ajar, trapped on an ankle with the foot sitting in the hallway. 87113's face shifted into a frown. They slid the door open, finding the room filled with unresponsive cybes. The 87364 whose foot had been trapped in the door sparked like someone had ripped wiring out of the body. 87113 reached out instinctively, stumbling into the blank space where the communal databank should have been. Searching for answers, seeking solutions.

A shaky breath ricocheted around in their lungs.

Alone.

It wasn't a question anymore.

They tucked the 87365's leg inside the room and stepped back into the corridor, limbs loosening with more time aware.

Slipping into another room they found a GH623 twitching like a broken graphics chip needed replacing, no longer able to move around for not being able to perceive the space. 87113 crouched and pressed fingers to GH623's face.

He jerked, spasming under the light pressure.

87113 retreated. A strange sensation built up in their chest, like their emotional surge-block chip was due an upgrade.

What could have caused this? What could have left at least the vast majority of 87113's fellows completely unresponsive?

Had the orbit run through an electromagnetic field? Had the power surged and broken the Mainframe Connection Units? Had 87113 been through a surge like that before? But still no answers came. No communal databank. It was like 87113 was a blank slate and yet something else tugged at their circuitry. Something they wanted to call new that felt all too familiar, unique, and too much their own to truly be so.

With no other ideas as to what to do, 87113 followed the thrumming bass out onto the main floor. They were still functional, they could still do their job. And even if not, what else were they going to do?

The club was open at all hours; the majority of the staff were cyborgs who, obviously, didn't need sleep outside semi-regular charging times.

It was supposed to be every fourth cycle that they each plugged in to charge. A day cycle, a night cycle, a day cycle, and then charging on that night cycle. But sometimes they went longer, if a client specifically asked for them or if someone else was being repaired. 87113 was popular. They were highly requested. And it had been over fourteen cycles since 87113 had charged. Over fourteen day-night rounds since they connected manually with the Mainframe.

It wasn't their fault was it?

Whenever Gen-3 cybes manually connected with the Mainframe, they shared all they had learned since the last time they had done so. Gen-3 were designed to learn. Gen-3 were designed to share what they had learnt with everyone else who could access the communal databank.

The floor of the club was largely empty. A few cybes danced and loitered on the main stage, their cybernetic markers shining out in colourful lights that matched the swirling patterns of the overhead lamps. The raised, circular platform of plexi reflecting everything that shone onto it. The booths around the edges of the floor were empty, pale blue plexi-leather seats flashing with the same lights that lit the stage.

Behind the bar stood a Gen-2 cyb', their bald head showing the circuitry beneath, ticking away as it should. Reassuring. Steady. Familiar.

Where were the clients? Why were there so few cybes out on the floor? Shouldn't the last shift still all be here?

But 87113 knew why there were no cybes. The unresponsive bodies strewn across charging room floors. How long had this been going on before 87113 woke up in the first place? Was that why no clients were in the building?

On the stage, one of the cybes' lights dimmed and he slumped to the floor, lying in a crumpled heap on the stage. The other cybes looked at him and carried on with their tasks.

87113 stared. Were they not going to do anything? Were they not going to help him? Were they not going to find a way to charge him? Was nobody going to do anything?

Fear

Welcome To Death
Ravi

Ravi grabbed Blue's hand. They pulled him up the pile of rubble and into their 'ship. The door squeaked closed in a supremely un-reassuring way.

Compared to the Re-An centre, the dim interior of the 'ship struck Ravi as a little gloomy. Something in him supplied the image of a pure white 'ship filled with green-uniformed people bustling from place to place. Neatness and order. The way their movements flowed felt right even as heat washed through Ravi's head once again.

Where were all the other people required to make a 'ship of this size run? It wasn't exactly a two person shuttle. The pilot's bay stretched up and around Ravi with several empty stations, each one of which had its own chair and blinking console lights. A bench ran along one wall where Blue slouched, having already tossed the white jacket unceremoniously into a random pilot's chair. They wore a sleeveless skin-tight black shirt and separate arm-sleeves that covered them from wrist to bicep. Past Blue, opposite the primary pilot's console was a closed doorway to the rest of the 'ship. Sleeping quarters and the mess – not that Ravi could say why he knew that.

Somebody sat in the primary pilot's chair, their hands appearing as they set the 'ship into motion. "Can't you be even a little tidy?" the pilot called. That must be the Petite that Blue had called to. "Rather than throwing your carefully sourced clothing around."

"Shut up," Blue grumbled affectionately. "It didn't even fit."

"It could easily fit someone else."

"Yeah, that'll come in *real* handy."

The pilot laughed.

Ravi stood by the door, as if frozen. What had he been thinking? He had followed the self-claimed Resistance onto their 'ship instead of waiting for his own transport to arrive. Now he would never find out why he had been Re-Animated in the first place! Not to mention the illegality of the situation.

Once the 'ship passed out of the range of Re-An centre sensors, the pilot emerged from the console.

She was short, barely reaching Ravi's chest. Her hair fell to her waist in soft waves and curls, pulled back by a piece of scrap fabric wrapped around her head. A scar slashed her left cheek, a sharp line that accentuated her cheekbones. She wore a sleeveless shirt similar to Blue's except far looser fitting and in a dark blue colour, and trousers that matched Blue's so perfectly that Ravi was half convinced she'd taken them out of Blue's wardrobe.

She shot a pointed look at Ravi's right hand. It was forming and releasing a fist again. Why was it doing that? Why couldn't he make it stop? His breath tried to hitch at the helplessness that swept through him.

"What's up, Re-An?" she asked, voice rough as if she'd spent a lot of her life shouting. "Rush job?"

"How would I know?" His voice came out a weak whine. He cleared his throat. "And it's Ravi, not Re-An."

"Petite." She held out a hand.

Ravi went to shake it only to find his wrist grabbed and a scalpel plunged into his skin. All too late he noticed the tool belt slung low on Petite's hips.

No pain followed the cut. Petite pulled back the neatly cut slice. Synthetic skin. He had synthetic skin. How had he not realised?

Blue glanced up from the porti-screen they had started scrolling through, and laughed. "Never trust an ex-mechanic not to mess with your circuits."

"That would have been useful to know before it happened." Ravi couldn't watch the way Petite fiddled with his insides. He knew it wasn't all human anymore, the doctor had said as much, but it was one thing to know and another entirely to be faced with it in graphic detail.

"They did a real number on you," Petite muttered. "This is shoddy work." She glanced up at Ravi's face, eyebrows low over her eyes. "They must have wanted you back particularly badly."

Ravi shrugged. He had no idea.

"Don't worry," Blue said without looking up as Petite returned to messing with his circuitry in a way that made jolts of pain like static shocks jump up Ravi's arm. "Petite can fix anything. You'll be all better in no time."

"I think I might be sick," Ravi muttered.

"Aim away from me please," Petite quipped.

"Can I sit down?"

Blue swore.

"What's up?" Petite asked.

"Files are encrypted."

"Run a decryption," Ravi suggested.

"Yeah," Blue sighed. "But which one."

"Military 5.2?"

"I don't know what that is."

Without thought, Ravi explained the format of the encryption decoding.

"You light up like a 'ship on fire when you do that," Petite muttered as Blue typed the decryption into their porti-screen.

"Well, call me an automata!" they cried. "It worked. And, more interestingly, I found someone."

The screen behind Ravi lit up. He shifted to look at it, arm still clamped in Petite's grip.

The colonel's hat did nothing to disguise his nose, far too large for the rest of his face. Nor did it disguise the emptiness in his eyes. His broad shoulders were cleanly defined by the perfectly pressed uniform jacket. He must have worked hard to gain a musculature like that, most military personnel didn't manage such musculature since gravity levels were at the discretion of the Station, meaning barracks and bases set their own gravity levels.

"Pilot," Blue read. "Colonel in the H4H squads."

"H4H?" Ravi asked.

"Humanity for Humans," Blue scoffed. "It's the faction that wants to ensure cybes don't get human status."

"That doesn't sound right..."

"You don't have much room to talk," Petite interjected, pressing his synth skin back into place. "You apparently worked for them."

"What are you talking about?"

"Cut him some slack," Blue said, obviously not having heard Ravi. "Everybody makes bad decisions sometimes, you and me included. Give him room to grow."

"I s'pose you're in a weird situation now," Petite said to Ravi. "Re-Ans are still a grey area when it comes to how human they are. Because Re-Ans were human once, but you did, you know, die so..."

"I worked for H4H?"

"Yeah." Blue gestured up at the screen showing the colonel. "That's you."

Colonel Simtiv. Date of Death: C.Aurora52.190

The world around Ravi swam.

"Blue, he's gonna crash!"

He'd been following orders.

Simtiv wasn't sure he believed in the cause exactly, but it was his job so his own beliefs didn't much matter. They were doing this to avoid a war, to avoid all the dangers presented by the only logical route the enemy would take. That was what the General had told him.

Nobody wanted a war. But the cyborgs hadn't given the humans any choice. These beings, these machines lived forever on solar power; they couldn't be left in charge. They would exterminate all organic life, would see humans as inefficient and not worthy of resources. It didn't matter that humans had created them, and hadn't Simtiv seen the Terminator movies?

Simtiv wasn't exactly sure how to explain to the General, or other people, that fiction and reality were different things and, just because something was explored in a fictional setting didn't mean that exact thing was about to happen in reality. Not to mention that the Terminator movies had been made originally when all humans still lived on Earth and could only travel as far as their moon.

His unit had been sent to bomb the supposed Cyborg Rebellion headquarters. The General had used the word 'probable' but in his years with the forces, Simtiv had learnt that 'probable' usually meant the information had come through whispers, rumour, and gossip, which lined up more neatly with 'supposed' in Simtiv's mind.

Either way, he had flown the approach, preparing to take out the Station. They hadn't expected much by way of resistance. Wow, had they been wrong.

The memory of the pain as the right side of his body had been crushed brought Ravi back to the moment at hand.

Petite stared down at him, sweat dripping from her face, a bloody chip held triumphantly in her hand.

A fizzle of static shock shot through Ravi. Blue collapsed back against the wall with a thud. They groaned long and low.

Petite dropped the chip unceremoniously on Ravi's chest and scrambled over him to kneel at Blue's side.

"I told you not to expend too much energy," she scolded. "What are we going to do now? If we plug you in to charge, you'll connect to the Mainframe and we'll be found, or worse."

"Maybe if you actually made that portable charger you keep promising," Blue's tone was easy-going, almost teasing.

"What...?" Ravi mumbled, mouth not wanting to obey him and form the words, head fuzzy with confusion.

"We took out your memory chip," Petite clarified. "Because it was going to fry out your brain. You're probably going to end up with a whole host of complications but you've survived re-living your own death so I guess you're tough enough. You're one of a kind, Ravi. Welcome to the Resistance, I guess."

Welcome To Redundancy
Dr Palmer

Dr Palmer stared at her front door. Dr Lazul bid her a good night and disappeared into her own suites. It had used to be a good thing that Dr Palmer was housed with the other scientists on the project. It had used to be a good thing that she didn't need to find her own accommodations somewhere. It had used to be a good thing that her commute was exactly the same as everyone else's.

Now she didn't know how she was going to escape. The camera in the corridor whirred as it spun toward the heat signature that was Dr Palmer standing outside her own door.

With a measured exhalation, she swiped her wrist against the door lock. It chimed open and she stepped inside. That was another thing to consider – her sub-dermal chip that she'd decided was *so much more convenient* than wearing a wristband. How could she have been so naive!

She changed her clothes, swapping out of her uniform outfit and into more casual clothes. She stuffed a few pieces of her life into a messenger bag – not large enough to carry much, not large enough to arouse suspicion, but big enough to shove her favourite tool belt into.

She hesitated again in front of her door; the cameras would see her exit. She needed a plan to move around unseen, or at least unnoticed. How could she make herself less noticeable?

If she had been living on her parents' Resi still, she would have been able to grab some shopping bags and just disappear that way, but the company delivered all the food she could need, so that wouldn't be possible. That had used to be a good thing too, the food delivery, allowing Dr Palmer to avoid having to think about getting food, freeing her mind to think more about her work or downtime.

Maybe her parents were the answer though. She grabbed a porti-screen. It took less than a minute to sabotage the Mainframe connection sensor. Dr Palmer dialled a call to her parents. When it couldn't connect, she made a little ruckus and dialled again.

She fixed the connection sensor and flung the porti-screen down on a table in a haphazard fashion. Muttering about her foolish parents and how she hoped nothing bad had happened to them, she scurried out the door.

She hesitated outside Dr Lazul's door, as if debating whether to tell her anything, then shook her head and said aloud. "No, I'll be back before the evening's over. No need to stress her."

She felt the fool for all her pretences. Would anyone even check the camera feeds? Would anyone even want to look for her? Would anyone even care that she was gone?

Nikolai would.

Thanks to Dr Palmer's job with Nikolai, the rest of the Palmer family now lived on one of the more middle class

Residential Stations, a step up from the hexi Dr Palmer had grown up on and into a pent. It was, however, inaccessible without having to transfer at a hub. The post-work rush kept the hub busy and bustling enough that Dr Palmer managed to slip onto the wrong transport, discarding her jacket and pulling a hat onto her head in an attempt to further disguise her travel.

By the time she disembarked the third transport, it was getting quiet enough that it might have started getting suspicious if she boarded another. Her heart thundered against her ribcage, beating so loudly in her ears that she could barely hear the tannoy system overhead. She slipped out of the transport hub, through the main square, and into the library.

Clinging to the edges of the building, she dipped into the bathroom, closing herself inside a stall until the lights dimmed to their night cycle setting. Thankfully she wasn't about to get tossed out for library closure thanks to the cybrarians at the front desk.

The datachip was burning a hole in her fist by the time she could pry off the end of her favourite screwdriver and set the chip inside it. Recognisable or not, Dr Palmer wasn't ready to give up her carefully curated tool belt or any of the tools on it.

This library was set out like every other library she had ever seen: her childhood Resi's library, her university Resi's library, even her current – or recently abandoned Resi's library. A ramp to automatic, clear plexi doors. Inside was the initial reference desk, clearly visible from the outside. The bathrooms were, always, to the left of the desk but had two entry/exit doors, one near the front of the building and one nearer the back.

The actual library floor had sections for working, desks of various heights and styles spread out, some completely enclosed by walls for privacy and lack of distraction, others in groups for communal studying or relaxation. There were even some shelves for physical copies of books and games, though this library had a particularly sparse collection. It figured in a pent. Hexi's were worse off than even that.

By the time Dr Palmer felt comfortable emerging via the rear bathroom door, sneaking into a secluded corner, picking up a discarded porti-screen as she went, the adrenaline was starting to shift into exhaustion.

She tucked herself into a corner near the back, far enough from the entrance that she shouldn't be visible to any late night visitors. She didn't want to risk drawing the attention of being in a library so late, let alone on a Resi that wasn't even hers.

Encrypting her actions was easy enough, pretty much every teen with a local Resi library – which was pretty much every teen in orbit – knew how to encrypt their data lest their parents request the logs and find out just how much smutty fanfiction they were reading. Thankfully, that also meant Dr Palmer's actions wouldn't stand out too badly.

The records database was freely available to access too, so Dr Palmer pulled up the records for her DNRA case. Pink Drabufly: aneurysm. Sad way to go, more so for anyone she left behind, but it seemed Pink Drabufly had been as insular as Dr Palmer herself. Housed in a hexi-flat, colloquially known as 'singles accoms'. No listed partner, no dependants, and her parents had died young too. Poor thing appeared mostly alone, all the more reason to request a DNRA; who was she going to come back to?

She whispered her apologies to the dead, to this woman whose life would have matched Dr Palmer's own if not for Nikolai. "May you return to the soil and replenish our futures." At least it was better than being forcibly Re-Animated.

It shouldn't have been that easy to set up a false identity. It should have been harder to shift the records around. It should have been more of a challenge to manage to disappear from the face of the Mainframe.

Dr Palmer – or Pink, she supposed – sidled around the edges of the library, shifting through the shadows of shelves, heart thundering in her chest once again, until she reached the nearest cyborg.

It didn't register her presence, designed to be approached from the front. It only had limited capacity, being a Generation-1. Pink pulled her favourite screwdriver from her tool belt and unscrewed the back of the cybrarian's head. She fished out its eye-processor and ducked underneath the station it manned.

She rewired the eye-processor to allow it to wipe her subdermal identity chip. Better to have no identity at a mechanical glance than her own. At least that way she could pretend to be Pink Drabufly without totally smearing the poor woman's memory.

It burned, lancing pain up her arm. She clamped her teeth around her lower lip to keep from making noise. Pained noises would draw the attention of the other cybrarians and Pink couldn't afford such a risk. Protocol would demand they call for medical attention, possibly emergency services. And then Pink would have to explain the damage to her arm and her subdermal chip. Not to mention the risk of medical staff figuring out something was wrong with Pink's attempts to create her false identity. Let alone if the cybrarians registered the damage Pink had done to one of them, that would result in them calling Keeping The Peace Officers.

With tears leaking down her face, Pink set the eye back in its socket, re-screwed the cyb's head together and snuck back to the bathroom to wait for the daylight cycle to start.

She tucked herself away in a random middle stall – nobody ever wanted the middle stall – and cradled her painful arm to her chest.

Oh shit.

What was she thinking! How could she possibly believe any of this was a good idea?

So what if she didn't think Re-Anning a DNRA was morally right? Who was she to start deciding on morality? She was an engineer; it was all she was, all she could be.

What the fuck was she meant to do for the rest of her life?

Welcome To Panic
87113

The regular transport appeared in the club docking bay once again.

All the bodies had been cleared out. All 87113's friends tossed into the body of a transport by humans in blue maintenance jumpsuits, piled atop one another and disappeared somewhere beyond 87113's reach. 87113 knew better than to assume they would ever find out what had happened. They knew better than to think too hard about the possibilities.

This transport was branded with the club's logo: a stylised trio of bodies dancing and writhing together in silhouette. It was the same transport that 87113 was used to seeing coming and going on a regular basis. Usually it was packed with humans, who spilled out of it even before the airlock had fully secured behind them. This time only a few humans emerged. Not many. Enough to keep the club going. Not too many for the scant number of cybes still available.

One approached 87113. A sadistic grin spread over his face, teeth shining out from behind the short beard that coated the bottom half of his face. He'd left his military jacket behind this time, the white short sleeved shirt beneath clinging to his muscles in a demonstrative way. Who was he trying to impress in this club?

But maybe he wasn't trying to impress here. Maybe he had been trying to impress elsewhere only to find himself here when that had failed.

And by the way his fingers bit into 87113's arm as he grabbed at them, 87113 knew their guess was accurate. He wanted to play with force, to claim what nobody was willing to give him freely.

Instinctively, 87113 reached for the communal databank, the ability to get lost in there and allow their physical form to perform the duties set out by their human client.

But there was no communal databank anymore. 87113 couldn't disappear and let their body run on autopilot. They had to stay in this moment, respond appropriately to this client that they hadn't chosen and didn't like.

No.

87113 didn't want to do this.

87113 didn't want to be alone with *this* human.

Not again.

Not this time.

But what could they do?

Their emotional surge-block skipped and fizzled in their chest, like too much current was blasting through it. It should have shut them off, but every other time 87113 had, intentionally or otherwise, retreated to the communal databank. Their body had learnt not to shut down in the wake of an emotional surge. But now there was no communal databank to escape to.

"No," 87113 whispered, unintended, accidental.

"Oh," the human chuckled. "You want to play that game with me?"

"No," 87113 repeated, firmer this time.

"You can play coy, but we all know what you want." His breath washed hot and wet over 87113's synthetic flesh. "We both know you were made for this."

The truth. This was what 87113 had been built for. It was why they looked and felt and behaved exactly like a human should other than the pair of blue bands wrapped around their forearms. This was their purpose. And it wasn't bad. 87113 didn't feel the need to retreat from every client. Some were even enjoyable.

But not this one.

Not now.

Not like this.

"I don't want to do this."

Harsh fingers wrapped around 87113's throat. If they were human they would have bruised with the force of it. But 87113 wasn't designed to bruise. "What is this *I* nonsense? You do as I tell you, 'borg!"

87113's emotional surge-block rattled, sending noises up into their ears. The tick-click and buzz of sparks jumping and rattling. A bad noise. That kind of noise could lead to a mechanical fault and 87113 had no doubts any mechanical faults would lead to them being piled in the back of a transport next time, regardless of how awake and aware they were.

The human's leg pressed between 87113's.

No.

No no no.

Their first whipped out and into the human's nose. Under their synthetic flesh and metal bone structure, the cartilage crunched, blood vessels ruptured.

He stumbled back, away from the assault, hands coming up to cover his nose. His face twisted into a mask of rage. Bright red blood spilled down onto his lips and into his beard.

87113's emotional surge-block continued its unsteady rattle.

Over the client's shoulder, the door to the transport was closing, ready to depart to pick up more clients and return them to the club.

The client reached out to grab 87113.

They bolted.

The transport's door slid closed with a hiss of pressurised air as it took off from the docking port.

The blood-stained human gestured wildly in 87113's direction, mouth moving in an obvious shout.

Soon enough, though, 87113 was too far to see through the small window. The club was just one small cube floating in the utter brilliance of a star system built by human ingenuity and mechanical skill. Instinctively, 87113 reached for the communal databank to seek out information on the creation of the system.

No databank.

They sank into one of the seats of the transport, the grey plexi-leather squeaking awkwardly under their weight as it released some of the air that had inflated it.

A mechanical voice announced their imminent arrival at a residential station. 87113 surged to their feet, clutching their arms to their chest, covering the blue bands that denoted them as a cyborg with their hands, one still painted red with the evidence of their actions.

The residential station was unlike anything 87113 had ever seen before. Beyond their wildest imagination, even with the now-lost central databank. Towering screens flashed with images and videos. Announcements from the government, advertisements for businesses, local information. Pretty humans signing and mouthing statements with captions written below. If there was sound to go with it, 87113 couldn't pick it out above the noise of the people utilising the port.

A cyb' that looked uncomfortably like 87113 smiled and winked at the people passing below. Unlike 87113 this cyb' had eyes that rivalled the blue of their bands. The camera zoomed away from them to show their body moving in a spiral around a silver pole. Two other cybes appeared at each side of them, each engaged in their own dance as the camera zoomed further away. The lights changed, silhouetting the three cybes and the name of 87113's club appeared below the image.

Dazed, 87113 let the crowd lead them into the main square of the residential station.

Someone had left a jacket on one of the plethora of benches, this particular one under a well-tended tree. With a quick glance around, 87113 slipped the jacket on, covering their bands and leaving their hands free. Hopefully nobody would notice them. Hopefully the owner of the jacket wouldn't come back. It didn't seem to be personalised or job-designated as far as 87113 could tell, but their experience was lacking, especially without the communal databank.

87113 sank down onto the bench.

Were all such places so green? Squares of moss-lawns littered the area, pretty purple and white flowers popping up from inside them. Hives for bees stood, protected by yet more moss lawns and plexi fences.

Trees stood tall and proud at each of the corners, markers for the entrances and exits of the main square.

Each well-tended and carefully trimmed. Healthy. Well cared for.

87113's emotional surge-block clicked in their chest. They had never been allowed anywhere this... alive.

Over the tops of the trees the docks' video screens played their adverts, flickering through their various images and videos.

People walked through the main square, passing 87113 without a second glance. All forms of humans going about their daily lives, something else to which 87113 had never been privy. Tall ones, short ones, adult ones, young ones – theoretically 87113 had known young ones existed, but they were so small! How could anything that small survive on its own?

But when one fell and its designated adult scooped it up, comforting the tears that leaked from its eyes, 87113 realised, they didn't. Humans didn't survive alone. Not the young ones, not the old ones.

Humans built communities. Everywhere, even in the ways they bumped into one another, stepped back, and apologised. Shared smiles and hand waves with total strangers.

"Come on, Blue," the adult comforting the child said. "Let's go home and get some dumplings, yeah?"

The tiny human sniffed and offered a teary smile. "With broccoli?"

"If that's what you want."

It was nothing like the communities 87113 was used to. Nothing like the sharing of thoughts and knowledge, nothing like a communal databank. But it was the same. And 87113 was all the more alone for it.

They should move. The human they'd run from could

arrive at any time. They needed to be gone when that happened. As they pushed to their feet, the same advert took over all the screens at once. This one did have sound 87113 could pick out.

"Do you have a malfunctioning Third Generation Cyborg?" an attractive woman with deep brown skin asked, words spoken aloud, signed and captioned all at once. Someone like 87113 appeared in the background, a typical service bot not designed with quite the same number of human-like features as 87113 themself. This one had sparkling green bands, lips, and hair in semi-solid braids. The braids moved with a head twitch – a simple enough fix, just loosen the neck connection to free up the pseudo-spinal column. "Don't forget, your beloved government will replace any malfunctioning Third Generation Cyborg completely free."

Replace?

"And if you're worried about your old one, don't be." The woman laughed. "They'll be recycled and fixed up into the newest generation of cyborgs. Generation Five is coming and it'll be our best yet."

87113's emotional surge-block clicked again. Uncomfortable. They rubbed a hand against their chest. That didn't bode well.

"Gotta wonder why they're so obsessed with this," one passing human said to another. "That ad has been playing on repeat for weeks."

"Maybe they just really want to provide the best quality cyborgs," their companion said.

The first human scoffed. "Does that sound like this government to you?"

"What else could it be, though?"

Resist

Welcome To Resistance
Ravi

The landing was rougher than Ravi might have liked, but not everyone could be a pilot – not that he remembered it, at all.

Petite had sat, worrying over Blue for the remainder of the flight until the 'ship had beeped to alert that they had reached the co-ordinates Petite had input. Petite had demanded Ravi keep an eye on Blue before heading up to the console to guide them into the Resistance base – wherever that was.

The door of the 'ship puffed as it opened, reacting to the change in air pressure. To Ravi's surprise, Blue pushed to their feet without aid. They emerged from the 'ship before Petite had finished docking, before the door had fully opened, before the docking plank was truly extended.

Ravi hung back, peeking through the open door to find a huge grey-ish docking bay spread out before him. Other vehicles littered the bay in states Ravi would generously title as 'battered'.

Blue's hips swung as they descended the unsteady, unanchored boarding ramp. A pink-haired woman with a mechanical left leg stood at the base of the ramp. Her scowling face did not enamour Ravi to the idea of leaving the 'ship. Flickers of something akin to memory overlaid the faces of equally scowling generals and other superiors in the military, none quite clear enough to fully make out, no specific circumstances to make the way Ravi's chest flooded with adrenaline make sense.

Petite clapped a hand on his shoulder and he flinched.

"Come on," she invited him off the ship and he trailed after her, feeling more like a lost child than anything else. What had he been thinking boarding a strange ship with someone calling themself The Resistance?

But he was here now and there was nothing to be done about decisions already made.

"This isn't exactly what we were looking for, Blue." The pink-haired woman swiped her fingers over the porti-screen Blue had been flicking through on the ship. The one that contained Ravi's personnel file.

"This is everything they had, which means what we want is in there we just have to find it. And, let's be honest, Toria, I guarantee nobody else would have done a better job. But you're welcome to go on the next mission yourself if my efforts aren't to your satisfaction." There was little of the jovial and friendly Blue that Ravi had become so quickly accustomed to in this conversation.

Toria pursed her lips and turned her body toward Petite, stopping when she noticed Ravi. She assessed him. Ravi's right hand formed and released a fist – oh, that was a new feature. Petite's meddling had only made him aware of it.

"And," Blue beamed. "This is Ravi."

Toria grabbed Blue's forearm and dragged them a few steps away, far enough for some semblance of privacy, not far enough that Ravi couldn't hear them. "You can't just pick up every stray you want and bring them here!"

Blue's response was lost to him, but it caused Toria to press her lips together again. She spun to face Petite. "I expect you in my office in twenty." With that she strode off.

Great, he wasn't even wanted here on this poor, impulsive decision. It wasn't like he could just go back to the Re-An centre since Petite had meddled with his memory chip.

"Don't mind Toria," Blue said, rolling their eyes.

"She's always like that," Petite added.

"It's hard for her. She's the person who always stays here, which means she's the default for managing everyone's missions and suchlike."

"She has Isa," Petite cut in.

Blue took on a distance that made Ravi think of other soldiers reliving trauma, glassy eyed and blank face.

"So, am I welcome?" he asked. "Or do I need to find my way back to the rest of the world?"

Blue laughed. "Come on, I'll show you around."

"You need to conserve power," Petite argued.

Blue waved a dismissive hand. "I'm fine. I know my own levels."

"You can't blame me for worrying about you."

"Petite, I swear–" Blue stopped and let out a huge breath. Their voice came out softer, "I promise I'll be careful, is that okay?"

Petite pouted but didn't say anything more.

Blue pressed their lips against hers.

Ravi jerked his head to look away, to give them privacy. How had he not picked up on that in the ship?

"I promise," Blue whispered.

"I just worry."

"I know. But you need to learn to trust me about this."

Petite sighed. "Yeah. I know. I'm sorry."

Blue nudged into Ravi's left, organic side. "Come on, you'll inevitably be hungry. People always are."

Petite sidled away, following a different corridor out of the docking bay to the one Blue began to lead him down.

Welcome To Protest Pink

The next morning, Pink emerged from the library as a group of teenagers entered – presumably on a project for school to be hanging around this early. She slipped around the early morning crowd with ease. Nobody would notice, but her heart had still invaded her throat. Maybe it just lived there now.

She loitered in an alleyway off the main square, trying to decide on a course of action. Where could she go? What could she do? How would she survive in the wake of this? She had no identity, at least not one that would stand up to scrutiny. And what would she even attempt to say? That she lost her wristband? Who would believe that?

She needed to leave this Resi at the very least. The risk of Nikolai seeking her out, searching for pings from her subdermal chip and sending someone to look for her here was too great. Okay, that was a plan then, sneak onto a transport to another Resi and make a proper plan from there.

In the centre of the main square, standing and blocking most of the pathways as well as the area used by parents doing things like teaching their kids to ride bikes, but not straying onto the moss lawns, stood a group of protesters. Masks hid the lower halves of their faces. They held and waved shattered plexi-board signs, obviously taken from construction sites and recycling yards. Each sign had a different slogan plastered across it in a variety of colours. Even from this distance, Pink could spot the theme.

Humanity For Humans was bad. People deserved rights, regardless of whether they had mech' or not.

Pink couldn't fault the argument: humans were human regardless of whether they required mech' to live – like her own mother's cybernetic lungs. Or even if they just wanted mech' enhancements – like her father, who had augmented his eyes to magnify for surgical purposes. But humans had those rights, nobody was trying to take them away as far as Pink had ever seen.

Humanity For Humans was just another noisy political entity, they wouldn't actually change anything. Things had been running the same way for generations.

But what else could these people want? To give Cyborgs rights? That made no sense, especially after the fiasco that had been The Crash. Not that Pink new all that much about that, too busy fiddling with circuit boards to pay much attention to irrelevant things. Human error, certainly, someone would have tried to install an update in the Mainframe Connection Units and not noticed the fry code they'd included or something. How else could it have happened? But why would these people argue that? Cybes were no more human than the light cycles systems.

Were they protesting the Re-An programme? Pink could hardly say Re-Ans were treated like regular humans after all, even without Nikolai expecting her to ignore a DNRA. She'd justified it by her figurative distance: she'd only worked on the mechanic side of it, not the interaction side. She'd justified it with the thought that Nikolai knew what he was doing. She's justified it by pure apathy. By ambition and the desire to work on cutting edge technology.

A squirming feeling set up in her stomach, as if her insides didn't want to associate with her any longer.

Military personnel approached the protesters, easy to spot even if the uniform had changed somewhat since the last time Pink had seen them. Still the same deep green – noticeable in the white walled Resi. But now they had the interlocking double H of Humanity For Humans on their sleeve.

While the military personnel had their hands up and empty, showing they didn't hold any weapons, Pink wasn't fooled. The military always had weapons, even just a switch knife posing as a multi-tool in their pocket.

Pink had seen it all too many times in her childhood Resi. Military personnel taking offence to something, approaching with open hands, only to grab the person and whip out their blade. More so if the person in question fought back.

At any rate, the sheer number of military personnel compared to the number of protesters told a story all its own. The protesters were outnumbered three-to-one. There was no ending for this but a violent one.

Pink should turn away, should leave before the violence erupted. She couldn't risk being caught here in the aftermath. But her feet were welded to the floor.

"Rights for all automated peoples!" One of the protesters yelled, shaking a sign above their head that Pink couldn't make out.

"Come on, now," one of the soldiers said. "This doesn't have to end badly. Let's all agree to calmly put down the protest signs and get back to work."

"My partner is dying because H4H won't support automated life!" A second protester yelled.

A third, obviously panicked by the nearness of the soldier to her left, swiped at him with her sign. The board split in half, pieces of words flying toward Pink but shattering before she could read it. The swipes of red paint turned to blood in the street.

Pink ducked down the alley before the chaos truly broke out.

All people deserved the right to life and access to all the things necessary to continue in relative comfort. But she couldn't risk herself like those protesters. She was already on the run. And if Nikolai ever found her... it didn't bear thinking about.

And anyway, who didn't have rights to life in this day and age?

Welcome To Identity
87113

Everywhere 87113 went, the advert played. Return your Gen-3 cyborgs for replacement.

Residential stations, workplace docks, even on the transports themselves if they had screens available.

They tugged their stolen jacket closer around them as they wandered through a Resi, street after street with house after house on it, each one a carbon copy of its neighbour including the layout of the little gardens in the front.

It had been weeks since they had run from the club, weeks more since waking up from what they mentally called The Crash. Loneliness clung to them. Every interaction was a risk. Every stolen socket they plugged into in the public libraries and in quiet corners brought the risk of being spotted as they conversed with the Mainframe. Charging was, much like sleep, the most vulnerable time for 87113. The time they were least aware, the time it would take the most to get out of the area.

And yet, they had hardly had even a semblance of a run in with anyone. Nobody seemed to recognise them as a cyborg. Nobody even looked at them twice, all too invested in their own lives to bother with whoever they passed, even if that person was wired into something.

It wasn't until 87113 saw a human plug their prosthetic arm into the same kind of socket that it dawned on them, most humans thought that 87113 was just like that person. Not a cyborg at all but a person with mechanical enhancements or prosthetics that needed to be charged.

These hexi-Resi's were proving to be 87113's favourites. Everything was hexagonal in shape, the station itself as well as the houses and central areas on it. The little gardens in front of the houses tended to be well maintained vegetable patches more than the moss lawns that the more central quad-Resis typically had. Practicality appealed to 87113 more than picturesque prettiness.

One particularly decadent looking patch pulled 87113 to a halt. Colours bloomed across it, red and yellow and peeks of orange and purple under the rich red-brown soil.

87113 reached out to touch the vegetation. Leaves ranged from spiky to waxy, all teeming with life and energy.

The front door of the house slammed open, its owner emerging, silhouetted by the light. "What's your name?"

87113 froze, retracting their hand, searching their internal databank for a name. They could hardly use their numerical designation. The memory of that falling young one who wanted broccoli dumplings for dinner played at speed. "Blue."

"And what do you think you're doing?"

"Admiring."

The homeowner beamed at that, and proceeded to explain to Blue exactly how to tend to a garden such as this one. Each individual seed that had been planted, each piece of care taken with it.

While they had been conversing, a small shuttle trundled up the street, barely fitting through the gap – these streets were designed for people walking, not vehicles.

Blue turned their head to watch as a military pair in their unmistakable deep green uniforms emerged from within.

One of them checked a porti-screen before tossing it back onto the seat she had just vacated in the shuttle. As she lifted her head, Blue turned back to face the vegetable patch, keeping their attention fixed on the soldiers.

The pair of them approached the house next door, knocking against the plexi and calling out, "We're from the military recycling project."

Blue gripped the edge of one of the planters filled with vegetables. The plexi dented under their fingers. Shit shit shit. These were people whose entire job was to collect cybes like Blue. Blue would be recognised for what they were and get tossed into the back of that rattling shuttle that didn't quite fit into the street. And then Blue would be gone. Dead, they supposed. Recycled into something more useful and entirely less Blue.

The gardener they had been speaking to trailed off, watching the interaction as the door in front of the soldiers opened.

The family inside brought out a GH651, deactivated. A pair of adults struggling with the weight. If Blue hadn't been able to see the purple arms, they would have thought this a dead, human body.

The human stood the cyb' up on their front garden path, stepping away with an exerted exhalation.

A young one peered up from behind its caretaker's legs.

"Excuse me, what will happen to Violet?"

"That's what she named it," the caretaker clarified.

The military woman, the designated speaker of the pair, crouched down to meet the young one's eyes. "We'll take it to get fixed up, don't you worry."

The child, apparently satisfied, returned inside, quickly followed by its parents.

The military pair scooped the deactivated GH651 up, grunting with the effort. GH651 were dense, originally designed for things like commercial kitchen or warehouse work. They carried her down the path and tossed her in the cargo section of the shuttle. The woman pulled the porti-screen back out from her seat, pressing a few buttons.

Her partner shot Blue and the gardener a smile and a wave.

Blue made an attempt at a wave back, almost dazed at the proximity to danger.

He turned to his partner and muttered, "Doesn't it bother you to lie to kids like that?"

"Nah," the military woman responded easily. "Saves the parents a tantrum. Kids get so attached to the strangest things."

A shudder rippled down Blue's back, their cables fizzling inside them as the military personnel climbed back into their vehicle and disappeared back down the street. They didn't know what happened to the traded in cybes, but they knew one thing for certain: they could not afford to be caught.

The gardener shook their head. "Such a shame that."

"Oh?"

"There was nothing wrong with Daisy's Violet, just

another set of people pulled in by propaganda." They brushed off their hands. "If you're interested, I have more plants inside."

Blue's face broke into a smile. "I'd love to learn more."

"I'm Gok, by the way," the gardener said as he slid the door shut behind Blue. He led them through the plain interior of his house and into the kitchen.

The window in the front was covered with a blackout blind, the counter beneath it coated in planters filled with greenery. Freestanding halo-lamps stood over the plants, providing them with the light they needed for photosynthesis.

How nice it must be to be a plant, root systems intertwining with one another in constant communication, only needing simple light and water to survive.

Gok talked Blue through the plants he had, the way he had grown them, the plans he had to expand onto another surface of his already cramped kitchen.

"I'd do a lot for more space to grow..." he sighed. "But I fear it's a pipe dream."

"More space would be nice," Blue agreed.

"I hope you don't mind me saying," Gok spoke hesitantly. "But are you a cyb'?"

Blue stumbled back, Gok stood between them and the kitchen door. If they wanted to leave they'd have to push past him. Shit. They should never have come inside. They should have known better than to trust a human. "No," they sputtered the lie. "Why would you say that?"

"The way you move, the way you watch things. You look at my plants like you've never worked a day in the agriculture stations."

Agriculture stations? Instinctively Blue reached for the

communal databank, that wash of distress blasting through them when the space was still empty. They ran an internal search, what had they learnt since The Crash?

"Everybody who lives on a hexi has done a stint in the agriculture stations. It's part of our school work experience at this level of orbit."

"I'm not from a hexi."

"But you're not formal and fancy enough to be from a quadri or a pent."

Blue shifted on their feet. Push Gok aside, run down the hall, take a left, out the front door – unless it was locked – and they could be away. Disappeared into the depths of the station. Maybe they could hide in the air filters. Or on top of a roof. Somewhere humans couldn't get without tools.

"I only ask because I'm part of this little group. We see how things are turning with this animosity toward cyborgs and we're worried about where it could lead."

"Where could it lead?" Blue asked just to keep Gok talking. If he was talking, he wasn't calling for someone to take Blue away.

"The persecution of everyone with mechanicals, regardless of whether they're a choice or for survival."

Blue frowned. "Could it?"

"I know it sounds extreme, but these things always start out with small steps. First the destruction of cybes who may or may not be gaining sentience, second make it hard for people to upgrade their mechanicals." Gok shrugged. "It only gets worse from here. People who want to exclude certain types of people always end up extreme."

"And what's your plan exactly?"

"Resist."

History

Welcome To Second Chances
Ravi

In the few days since Blue had shown him the basics: mess, a room he could claim, and Petite's engineering lab, the corridors and communal spaces of the Resistance base had emptied out. When Blue had taken him into the mess, encouraging him to pile a plate high with fresh grown produce better than any he could remember tasting, the room had been bustling.

Without Blue to guide him, Ravi kept finding empty corridor after empty corridor. The communal areas were sparsely populated. Nobody ever seemed to be where Ravi was, or, in the few cases where they started there, it didn't last long.

He limped through the painted, empty hallways, breath rattling in his chest with the pain of each step. Why was nobody here? Where were they all? Were they hiding just to watch him squirm?

Would he even want a random Resistance member to help him right now? He's much rather find Blue or Petite, someone he trusted even a little.

He stumbled, crashing into a wall hard enough to bruise. Could he bruise on synthetic skin? His right leg bent of its own accord, yanking Ravi to the floor with a cry.

His heartbeat pounded in his ears, breath catching somewhere in his throat. His right leg wouldn't move. He was trapped. Alone.

Ravi's body started to shake all over. He tried to claw at his chest, to remove the pressure that stopped him from taking a proper breath. His right hand didn't respond.

Trapped.

His enemy would find him if he stayed here. Everybody knew they were merciless with the way they treated people, ripping them to shreds in the hopes of finding some tech they could use. And Ravi was all kinds of tech now. His entire right hand side was mechanical and who only knew how much else of him. He was ripe for the harvesting.

His left hand grabbed at his head, as if it could rein in his rapidly spiralling thoughts. The images circling around inside his brain.

Alone.

He had to move, to find a safe place. A place to hide out until he could get help. No, there would be no help. Ravi was on his own. He had to fend for himself. He tried to push off, to crawl even, but his entire right side was limp and gripping, crushing. Oh stars, he was going to die all over again.

Vulnerable.

He let out a scream but no sound came out. No air in his lungs. No breath. No help.

Trapped.

Alone.

A hand landed on his shoulder. A gentle touch that hit

with the force of a kick.

Ravi flinched. He peeled his eyes open. When had they closed?

Bright green cybernetic eyes blinked at him. "Human?" the person mouthed. Maybe they spoke; Ravi could hear nothing beyond the rush of blood buzzing in his ears.

He might have nodded.

The green-eyed person took Ravi's left hand in theirs and placed it against their own chest. Even breaths lifted and lowered Ravi's hand. She laid her other hand on Ravi's own chest, applying gentle pressure to match her own breaths.

Ravi's breathing slowly shifted to match the guidance. His heart still in battle with his ribcage.

"Just breathe." The voice was laced with a mechanical hum but at least it was audible now.

Ravi tried to focus on the idea that someone would have cybernetically enhanced their throat, but nobody would do that, would they? That meant this was a cyborg. Ravi's breathing sped up once again. If this was a cyborg, he was in their lair and he was definitely going to be harvested for parts.

Cyborgs would kill him.

"Whoa, hey, it's okay. Just need to breathe," the cyborg said, continuing the gentle pressure on and off Ravi's chest.

A soft touch. Ravi focused on that again, letting his eyes fall shut until he could get himself under control. He had joined the Resistance by choice of sorts, he was here by choice and he should have known cybes would be here too.

Finally, his panic subsided. He opened his eyes again, more prepared to take in the cyborg in front of him. The sides of her head were green panels, mechanics ticking away inside, but the majority of her face was exceedingly human. She wore a delicate floral shirt in shades of pinks and blues that tickled something just out of reach in Ravi's mind.

She twitched a smile. "There we go. Has this happened to you before?"

Ravi nodded. "Soldier," he huffed, breathless, throat raw.

The cyb' nodded slowly. "I know."

Fresh, hot tears rolled down Ravi's face. If this cyb' knew Ravi was a soldier, did that mean everyone on the base knew? Or did it mean he, in his Pre-An life, had done something horrible to this cyb'? Those panicked thoughts had certainly painted an anti-cyborg picture out of his instincts.

The cyborg shushed him and repeated the gentle pressure and breathing. Had she ceased to breathe when she wasn't coaching Ravi? "I'll take you to the medi centre."

Ravi shook his head. No, he didn't want to see a doctor, not after waking up the way he had in that Re-An centre. And the fear of being taken apart...

The cyb's pupils adjusted like a camera lens as she processed. "Do you have a person?"

"Blue."

"Of course it's Blue." She rolled her eyes. "Who else. Let me help you up." She scooted under Ravi's disobedient right arm, pulling is around her shoulders and holding his wrist tightly in place. "I'm Isa."

"Petite mentioned you," he breathed. "I'm Ravi."

With Isa's help, Ravi made it down several corridors and into a huge room, almost the size of the docking bay except where the docking bay was empty but for the five or so 'ships, this room was packed full of bits and pieces of machinery, tables filled with tools and circuit boards, and other similar engineering paraphernalia.

"Blue?" Isa called. "Petite?" She propped Ravi against a relatively empty table. "You okay?" she asked him.

Ravi nodded but it might have been a lie.

Isa turned away from him and called again. "Blue? Petite?" she wandered further into the crowded room. "Petite!"

"What?" Petite's called back, rough voice echoing in the space.

"It's Isa."

"I know who it is, I asked what you wanted. If this is about the porti-chargers, I haven't finished them yet."

"I want you to fucking come out and talk to me!" Isa snapped.

Petite's head popped up from what appeared to be some kind of engine. Her scowl morphed into a soft expression as she spotted Ravi, tear-stained and leaning painstakingly against a desk. She wiped her hands on a cloth half hanging out of her tool belt. "What happened?"

Ravi's breath hitched once as he tried to shrug. He ignored the way Petite's eyes traced the tear tracks on his face. "Rush job."

"He said Blue's his person. I figured they'd be here but..." Isa looked around at the noticeable lack of Blue.

"I can handle him."

Isa stepped close to Petite, whispering frantically.

Petite's face shifted from concern to a scowl and back again. She placed a hand on Isa's shoulder. "Second chances, right?"

Isa shot a final look at Ravi before heading back out of

the huge room.

Petite folded her arms and cocked a hip to one side. "Well, let's hear it?"

"My right leg – my whole right side."

"The whole thing, huh?"

"My–" his breath hitched again.

Petite's hand jerked out to touch his left arm, her hand ghosting over his bicep.

"My death flashback involved crushing."

Petite let out a low whistle. "Ambitious trying to bring you back." She sighed. "An ambitious rush job."

"Bad combination," Ravi agreed. "Pretty sure that's what got me killed too."

Petite barked out a laugh and covered her face with one hand, the hand that wasn't touching Ravi. She tapped at him with the hand still on his arm. "You can't make jokes when you're all damaged."

"I can and I will."

"Hop up on that table and let me see what I can do."

Welcome To Suspicion
Pink

Pink puffed out a breath, lifting the ever-lengthening hair out of her face for the briefest of seconds before it fell in front of her vision once again.

Dr Palmer: government engineer had kept her hair short. She'd had regular access to hair dressers and it had worked well for her to keep it out of her eyes when she was working on circuit boards and other mechanisms. Unlike Dr Lazul, she hadn't wanted to spend every morning plaiting her hair to keep it back, so a cute pixie cut had been the perfect choice.

Pink: fugitive in hiding didn't have that access. And, even if she had, she needed to make as many changes to her appearance as possible from Dr Palmer lest she be recognised. New clothes – or at least clothes that were new to her even if she had technically pilfered them. Instead of her well fitted legging and formal shirts, she'd grabbed an oversized dress with a too-tight jumper tied around her waist both as a belt and to disguise the tool-belt she knew was too distinctive but couldn't risk giving up. If her screwdriver with the chip got into the wrong hands...

She'd been on the run for several weeks at this point, catching what sleep she could on cross-Resi transports and in the quiet sections of libraries, setting up films on porti-screens so it didn't look like she was the with the express purpose of sleep.

She'd had half a mind to let herself waste away like that until one random teen had dropped her porti-screen in front of Pink, who had scooped it up without thought, and fixed it.

The teen had thanked her profusely and offered up a mostly uneaten packed lunch. "It's not much but it was chilli day at school so... you look hungry."

The teen had jogged off home, leaving Pink with the satchel-looking lunch container and the easing of her painful hunger. That, and an idea.

Working as an under-the-table handyperson didn't pay well. Most payments came in the form of food, or somewhere to stay, but occasionally there was tech that Pink could trade. But there was always work to be found, particularly on the larger and poorer Resis.

She traded the few things she'd packed from her bag into the lunch satchel, dumping her old bag on a random transport she didn't even stay on, just on the off chance that someone recognised it.

Her bag that had once been a lunchbox hung heavy on her shoulders when she walked with it, weighed down with every possession she had manged to scrounge up along with all the hardware. It wasn't much of a calling, but it kept her going. Kept her alive.

This latest job was to fix a family's outdoor lights so they were controlled from inside rather than the Resi's day-night light cycles. It hadn't been the easiest conversation Pink had ever been a part of, her lack of fluency in sign was entirely her own fault – always too busy playing with circuitry and codes to pay much attention to language lessons in school. But she'd figured it out. It should have been done by a government certified engineer, but this far on the edges of orbit it was no surprise that nobody had come yet.

"Excuse me," a voice called from behind her as she resealed the panel she'd taken out.

She turned, maybe somebody else in the neighbourhood needed something too. The military uniform froze her where she stood. The colonel's hat sat low over his eyes, doing nothing to disguise the sheer size of his nose. Pink tried for flippant as she shoved her tools back in her bag and slung the strap over her shoulder – ready to run. "What's up?"

"I've had some queries about a suspicious person in the neighbourhood."

Great! The neighbours had reported her. Assholes. This was why she needed a better disguise.

She pulled a forged certification out of her bag, yet another library creation, and flashed it. The logo should be enough that this colonel wouldn't want to look her up in the database. "Just doing some maintenance."

The colonel frowned and stepped closer. Close enough for Pink to read the name stamped across the tag over his left shirt pocket, right over his heart.

"Can I see that?" Colonel Simtiv requested.

Pink pressed her lips together and held out the certification card. She examined the pretty garden for escape routes. It had been well tended, a small vegetable patch covered the left side, a wall of pea plants creating a boundary higher than the standardised walls. Not the best escape route.

Colonel Simtiv blocked the front path, so that was a no go. And to the right was a slightly higher wall, the end of this neighbourhood and start of the next. It was, however, only up to Pink's waist and across the small patch of moss lawn. She could probably make it over the wall unscathed. The real question was whether she could do it before Colonel Simtiv got hold of her.

Simtiv's hand slipped into his pocket, other reaching to pass the card back.

Pink reached out to grab the sheet of plasti.

Calloused fingers wrapped around her wrist. The card fluttered to the ground, settling in the moss like poorly irrigated rain systems that turned to shards of ice.

"I'm going to have to ask you to come with me," Simtiv said, voice firm.

Pink tried to wrench her wrist out of the colonel's grip but she might as well have been cuffed to a wall for all the good it did.

Her heart thundered in her chest, limbs tingling, brain whiting out.

If he took her in, she'd be exposed. All her stuff would be taken and, idiot that she was, she had written her full, original name on the inside of her tool belt.

They'd know who she was. And she'd be disappeared like Vedran or, worse yet, returned to Nikolai. She couldn't say why she knew that would be worse, she just did. Stealing from someone that powerful was always going to have been dangerous and something told her he would take great comfort in making her truly understand how much trouble she had put him through. Maybe that *was* what had happened to Vedran.

Next think Pink knew her teeth had dug into the hand around her wrist.

Colonel Simtiv cried out, free hand flashing out to shove at Pink's face.

Warm, wet blood filled her mouth just as pain sliced across her cheek.

They both stumbled back. Colonel Simtiv clutching his bitten hand to his chest, the blade in his non-bitten hand shining wetly with blood.

Pink clamped fingers to her bleeding cheek and bolted for the low wall into the next neighbourhood, leaving her fake credentials on the moss lawn where they had fallen.

"Colonel Simtiv on Residential Station 6B15, requesting assistance in Neighbourhood AF62J."

Welcome To Violence
Blue

Passing themself off as human was easy enough in a variety of neighbourhoods, each slightly too large to truly know whether someone belonged or not. The residents slightly too drained to bother finding out as long as the person in question wasn't doing anything bothersome.

The brief comment from Gok about quadris and pents being posher had given Blue enough to know to avoid lingering in those where they could.

They recognised their luck in not needing to sleep, especially as they saw humans chase off other humans from sleeping on benches in the main square of Resis of all types and sizes. They didn't bother to investigate too much, though, lest they get drawn in and labelled a nuisance.

They slipped into a library, settling themself by a charging port as the day light cycle changed to the night one. Their battery chimed internally that it needed attention.

With a quick glance around, Blue let their consciousness retreat inside to investigate as the wire found its connection point.

Whomp!

Their limbs fizzled, jerking to rigidity. Malleable to mannequin. Their central processors began to shut down in pieces, cutting their sight, their hearing, their perception of their own form.

Alerts sounded in their head, sounded across the central Mainframe. "Cyborg!" the alerts cried, and the designation for the area in which they were charging.

"Shit!" With fingers clumsy and still too rigid from the attack, they yanked the charging wire out of their arm and scurried from the library, pulling their jacket sleeves down to hide their arms.

It would be fine. Nobody was going to get here that fast. Blue would be gone before anyone who received the message arrived. And, even if they weren't, how would anyone recognise Blue as a cyborg without removing their jacket?

Over the next few days, military presence increased in the Resis Blue visited. Deep green uniforms standing distinct from the other greenery, like the trees and moss lawns. The uniformed officers peered at people, as if each one was worthy of suspicion. The humans ceased to linger in their own, open communal areas.

It became almost impossible to find a quiet place to charge at all.

After dipping down a random alleyway behind a building, Blue stumbled across an outlet. For what reason it had been put there Blue couldn't begin to imagine, but there was nobody else around to see.

Taking a deep breath they plugged into the socket. Once again the EMP-pulse shot through them, fizzling over their limbs and turning their head foggy and fuzzy.

Blue lingered as long as they could stand it, even with the alarms ringing in their head. Even with their location being blasted on a frequency – probably military.

It ached, it burned, and it definitely wasn't a one off bad socket. This was a virus. An active attack against people like Blue. But Blue had to endure or they would be without the power they needed to survive. And if Blue lost power, there was no way to protect themself from anything.

"Cyborg!" Someone roared, the voice carrying over the alarms in Blue's head.

They whipped around to see who had made the noise, yanking out the charging cable and shoving it into their pocket. Was it directed at them? Who else could it have been toward?

Their long hair, pulled into a ponytail atop their head whipped around their face, distorting the bland, white walls of the alleyway.

Someone latched onto their hair. Yanked their head back by the ponytail.

Some kind of habit tried to kick in, tried to make Blue pliant and complacent and giving. But it got stuck against Blue's newly developed personality.

The human tugged harder on Blue's ponytail. Blue stumbled to walk backwards. Their hands scrabbled at the plain and blemish-free walls. Nothing to grab. They tried to turn, tried to get a view of their assailant, but to no avail.

They grabbed at him, finding harsh canvas clothing. Trousers, shirt, belt. Pockets. Something in the pocket over his left hip.

Blue's fingers dug into the fabric, tearing it away from the clothing.

"Hey!"

But Blue clutched a multi-tool now. They extended the blade; it shone wickedly sharp in the overhead lights. But what next? Was Blue about to stab this human? No. That went against their programming, if that still played a part. And even if it didn't, was that really who Blue wanted to be?

The human grabbed for Blue's arm, fingers digging too easily into their synthetic skin, pressing against their circuitry in a way that made colours dance across their vision. That couldn't be normal.

Blue swiped the knife between the hand on their hair and their head. The hair came away in the human's hands, allowing Blue to swing around and face him, tethered by his grip on their arm.

He was in military uniform – minus one trouser pocket thanks to Blue. Bland, deep green canvas coated his entire form in matching buttoned shirt and trousers. He even had the hat, peak dipping low over his eyes but not hiding his impressive nose.

"Get back here!" he demanded, hand flailing out to grab at Blue's other arm, to grab at the hand holding the knife, even as his grip on the one he held tightened to the point of damage.

Is this what pain felt like?

"Let me go," Blue insisted, writhing in his grip, desperate to free themself, to run.

"You need to be reset. It's for your own good." His epaulettes shone gold in the changing light cycle as he yanked Blue ever closer. "Just come with me to the reset station."

"As if I'm going to do what you say after you grabbed

me out of nowhere!" Blue put the knife against their trapped arm. They could do without an arm, right? The fabric under the blade gave way, splitting easily. The human's grip loosened.

The sleeve of Blue's stolen jacket from that first step onto a Residential station tore easily now that one cut had been made. Blue yanked their arm out of the human's grip. They dropped the multi-tool and dashed down the alley, finding the same kind of small shuttle that had taken away the GH651 from Gok's neighbour. They scrambled into the seat, flicking buttons to turn it on.

Their emotion surge-block clicked in a haphazard fashion, making it hard to catch their breath – fuck whoever had decided Blue needed to breathe instead of just mimicking like all the other models of cyb'!

The military man stormed out of the alley, multi-tool in hand just as Blue pressed the button to make the shuttle blast forward and away from him.

Too fast. Almost too fast for Blue to even register. The shuttle blasted through the streets, bouncing off walls and rampaging over bushes until it shoved into the docks and straight out the other side, through the atmo-bubble, on the tail of a larger transport leaving the area.

The lack of gravity scrambled Blue's perception, lifting them and any other unsecured thing from the seats of the shuttle. Out the front window the stars expanded, distant and distinct.

Blue stared, mesmerised by the sight of it. Pinpricks of light creating cast and beautiful patterns just like circuitry. Was this the kind of thing that had inspired Blue's own creation?

The flightpaths weren't programmed into this shuttle.

It was never really intended to fly outside atmo. Blue was no pilot. Blue wasn't even pilot-adjacent. They pulled at the controls. The shuttle spun out of control, Blue rattling around inside it like the single sugar-coated-chocolate left in the tube.

At least they wouldn't be recycled.

With a brain-shaking thunk – could Blue call it brain-shaking since they didn't, technically, have a brain? – the transport crashed into something and stuck.

Blue blinked, reorientating themself with the new pull of gravity. They took a breath and reached for the door.

Carefully, Blue climbed out of the shuttle. Red soil stretched out in front of them, as far as they eye could see. A huge expanse of red soil. Was this an agricultural station? But no, above Blue were only the stars.

"What the fuck?" they breathed, surprised to find the words not sucked away into the vacuum of space. Was this a planet? An honest to engines planet? A planet with soil and an atmosphere, and enough gravity to stick Blue to its surface?

Blue sank to their knees, battered trousers catching the red dust. The dug their fingers into the ground. It shifted under their grip, giving way and particulating. They picked up a handful of dusty dirt. The same kind of dirt that Gok used for his planters.

If they planted something here, would it grow in this soil? Could bees survive in this atmosphere? Could humans live on this planet? Live without needing artificial stations orbiting the central Mainframe?

Even if they could, would Humans be able to adapt to living with no ceiling over their heads? Nothing visible between them and the endless sparkling darkness of an unobscured sky?

And then, would they let people like Blue, cybes like Blue live out here with them? Free people? Was it worth the risk of sharing?

Sometimes Blue wished they could cry. Humans had catharsis when they cried. Blue, however, had been programmed with emotions that had no apparent release.

Quietly, Blue let themself sink into power saving mode.

Connection

Welcome To Care
Ravi

"Blue," Ravi greeted as they walked into the huge engineering room. "You're back."

Somewhere in the mass of construction, Petite clunked and thunked her own efforts.

"Hi Ravi." Blue hopped up to sit on the desk next to Ravi's project – an old L52 engine part with shredded screw-heads that he was taking apart to see if there was anything useful left. It was hard work, would have been even without having to use his non-dominant left hand. Still, it had been something to do. Something to distract him from the pain and panic of that morning. "I hope you got permission to touch that. She can be a diva about mechanics."

"I did," Ravi laughed.

"How are your limbs? Isa found me, told me what happened."

Ravi rubbed his eyes with his left hand. The movement was weird and uncomfortable but infinitely better than the feel of his fake skin on his sensitive eyes.

"You don't have to tell me."

"Where have you been?" Ravi asked instead.

"I'm the go-to for away missions," Blue grumbled.

"Confidential away missions?"

"Always."

"I get that." Vague memories of lonely missions in a shuttle sized for a single person flickered on the edge of Ravi's thoughts. His right eye buzzed in his skull in a way that set his teeth on edge. "You took Petite on the Re-An mission, though."

"Pilot, planning, and engineering support. We couldn't dock our ship there because they keep more thorough records than most places."

"I suppose a Re-An Centre is a highly sensitive place."

"Exactly."

"So this time...?"

"Just me."

Ravi frowned.

"It's no big deal."

"You sure about that? Maybe it's a small deal?"

Blue pursed their lips. "Pretty rich that you're asking me that when you won't share."

"You don't have to tell me," Ravi parroted Blue's earlier words back at them.

They sighed and leaned backwards until their head hung over the other side of the desk. Their shirt rode up a little at their waist, revealing a flash of pale skin.

Ravi went back to tinkering but the silence hung heavy over the room. Uncomfortable. "You seem tired."

"One way to put it."

Ravi frowned. "What do you mean?"

"What do you know about The Crash?"

"It was... bad?" Ravi offered.

"It was the event that freed the cybes. Or evolved – it's

hard to explain. Either way, the government didn't like it. Do you remember the recall of the Gen-3 cybes?"

Ravi's mind clicked with the idea, as if he had heard something about it before, but he couldn't recall any of the details.

"A lot of humans listened to the recall – after all, all they knew was that their cybes weren't functioning as intended and the government promised to replace them."

"Right..." Ravi agreed, uncertain how this related to Blue and their tiredness.

"The people in power were shifting. The H4H policies started becoming more blatant and they put a bug in the Mainframe."

"A bug?"

"It alerts when a Gen-3 plugs in to charge, sends out a signal with the location of the charging cyb' on specific military frequencies."

Ravi's eye buzzed in his skull again. He pressed his organic hand against it. "I'm not sure I follow."

Blue exhaled a heavy breath. "It just makes charging more of a challenge."

Ravi nodded vaguely; it would be exhausting carrying around low battery tech. He'd heard from other soldiers with mech' that the low battery alerts were equally as draining as the weighty and depletingly useful mech' and that there was no way to turn them off. But if Blue was struggling that much with charging and using their mech', surely they shouldn't be going off on missions on their own. "Is there nobody else?"

"That's always my question too." Petite appeared from under an engine block.

"Where did you come from?" Blue asked, sitting up and

spinning on the desktop so they faced Petite.

Petite ignored the question, stepping up close to Blue and cradling their face in one oil-stained hand.

Blue leaned into the touch. "I'm fine," they reassured.

"You're tired."

"I'm always tired."

Ravi looked back down at the L52.

"You shy, Ravi?" Blue teased him.

"Just giving you privacy."

Blue snickered. "Why?"

"Hey!" Petite chided. "Maybe I like privacy. Not everybody is as chill as you about displays of affection."

"Who touched whose cheek here?" Blue's voice was filled with mirth.

A smile tugged at Ravi's lips and he risked a peek back up at the pair of people who had invited him into the Resistance in time to see Blue press their mouth to Petite's in a rapid pattern that had the woman squealing with laughter as she retreated.

"You're such a child!" she accused.

"Oh says you!" Blue shot back.

Petite stuck her tongue out at Blue.

Blue hopped off the desk. "I should go report back to Toria. She's gonna be pissed."

Petite wiped her hands on the cloth hanging from her tool belt, watching Blue retreat from the room, oil stained handprint still shining in the light.

"How long have you two...?" Ravi trailed off before he finished the question. Inter-military relationships were heavily regulated and generally frowned upon, if it was like that here he didn't want to put a name to it.

"I dunno," Petite answered, leaning against the desk

where Blue had so recently sat. "It happened so gradually, you know? Blue introduced me to the Resistance, helped me find my place in it. We just started spending time together and it... Just, sort of happened."

"All the best relationships are like that," Ravi said.

Petite grimaced. "Are we using the word relationship here?"

Ravi raised an eyebrow. "Are we not?"

"It just feels... reductive. We're not tied to one another, we just keep making choices. We both know the risks. We can't put one another above the mission. It's not..." She sighed. "It's just for fun. It's not serious."

Welcome To Kindness
Pink

The cut across her face would garner too much attention, which left Pink dashing into a library bathroom to rinse off the blood as best she could with what little time she had available considering she needed to get off this Resi before they locked down the docks. Not that the bleeding stopped. And, since this was a hexi, the hand dryers were air based rather than tissue or towel based, which left her holding a wad of toilet paper to her face as she scurried toward the docks only to find it teeming with green uniforms.

She aborted her movement so quickly that she stumbled into the person behind her. "Ah, sorry," she muttered, tilting her head down. They might not see the blood if she kept her head down. "I think I left my water running."

She rushed back through the commercial district, adverts blasting to either side of her. The alert banner appeared beneath them, the same green as the military uniform.

Person of interest: a woman wearing an oversized dress with a cut on her face.

She didn't bother to hang around and see what else popped up in the description of her, especially as a pair of military uniforms appeared at one end of the street.

She dipped inside a random textile stall in a random marketplace. The proprietor welcomed her with a wide smile that somehow seemed to spread to the mechanical half of his face despite the lack of synthetic skin to cover the mechanisms. He glanced behind her at the alert banner, mechanical eye buzzing audibly even in the noise of the district. He looked at the wodge of bloodied tissues pressed against her face, and invited her into the back.

For no reason she could name, Pink followed the man's lumbering gait through the thousand pieces of hanging fabric and into a small back room that had definitely been designed for employees to take their breaks in, and had clearly been used for far more than just that.

He invited her to sit at a black topped table and grabbed a first aid box from an annotated cupboard.

Without a word, he cleaned up the cut and bandaged it then washed his hands and served up a bowl of sticky rice and mushrooms. She dove on it, food soothing the painful ache in her stomach that seemed to be a permanent addition to her life these days.

"I know my food isn't that good," he teased when she was done. "You must have been really hungry."

Pink ducked her head.

"You fallen on hard times?"

"Something like that."

"Let's see if we can't find you some better clothes, yeah?"

Pink watched him retreat to another door, sliding it open to reveal a well-maintained bedroom. "Why?" she asked.

He turned that bright smile on her once again. "Because I hope someone will offer me the same kindness should I ever need it. I'm Star, by the way."

"P–" she cut off her old name as it tried to fly out of her mouth through habit alone. "Pink."

"Well, Pink, these should fit a little better than that." He handed over a folded pile of clothes. "Let me go make sure nobody is bothering my front of house. You stay here, and if the lights flash twice there's a hidey-hole under the sofa."

As soon as the door shut behind him, Pink surged to her feet. She took the time to change into the faded t-shirt and oil-stained jumpsuit before searching for potential exits. It made no sense that Star would clean her up, feed her, and offer up a hidey-hole only to rat her out immediately, but Pink was too used to her life on the run to truly believe someone would offer kindness, risk their own life with no promise of reward. No, she should find a way to leave quietly and disappear from this kind stranger's life.

In short order, Star returned, surprisingly alone. "We've been asked to close up for the day. Apparently the military are looking for someone."

Pink's heart leapt into her throat.

"Wouldn't say what for."

"I..."

"I never have trusted a rule without a reason." Star's mechanical eye made another whirr noise as it adjusted to the change in lighting.

"Is your eye bothering you?" Pink asked, fastening her tool belt around her wait instead of holding it in her hands.

"My eye?"

"It makes noise."

Star shrugged. "It's always done that, ever since I installed the slightly better quality one than the one I got issued. That thing had problems."

Pink pulled a screw driver from her tool belt. "Do you want me to...?"

"You can fix it?"

Pink smiled. "I'm good with my hands."

Star took a step back. "This is my vision we're talking about."

"I'm a qualified engineer."

Star examined her, sat at the table and gestured for Pink to have at it.

Welcome To Solitude
Blue

Wandering around the little planet, boots digging into the red soil in an oddly satisfying way, Blue stumbled across some of the things that had turned a clump of random space debris and soil into a gravity and atmosphere having planet. A 'ship lay partially submerged in the soil, unlike any 'ship from Blue's personal database. Solar panels coated its exterior hull, coated in a fine sheen of red dust. Blue brushed the dust away and found the machine still humming quietly.

Still alive?

They found the hull breach on the far side as they walked around the ship, dusting it off as they went. Slipping inside revealed old machinery. Gen-1 style machinery. This could well have been from the beginning of the Orbital Captaincy, when the travellers had decided to settle where they ended up rather than pushing to make it to their intended destination, or even before.

Dust coated the entire interior, soft soil coating the floor beneath Blue's feet. But lights blinked, one had been covered by a sign that read "gravity systems" and shone in a bright green. Another read "atmo" also green.

And below them, a charging port. It was old, ancient, but Blue pulled the charging cable out of their jacket pocket and, tentatively, clipped it into the battery unit.

It was hardly the same as a proper Mainframe Connection Unit, but Blue hadn't seen one of those in years now. It felt like nothing they had ever experienced, a vast emptiness – no connection to the Mainframe to be found. Something about it made Blue so desperately sad they almost wanted to let themself run out of battery and cease functionality right here. What was the point of life if you had to live it in this awful solitude? Instead they petted at the walls and told the 'ship it was good, that it wasn't alone anymore, even though they knew it couldn't process their words.

Battery charged to a more reasonable level once again, Blue headed back to the shuttle. There was no point hanging around here if they didn't have to. The shuttle's nose was buried in the dirt. First things first: digging that out. Second things second: running a diagnostic check. Third things third: figuring out how to get it off the planet and into an orbital pattern that would allow entry to a Station.

Digging at the soft soil seemed easy enough until Blue had been doing it all day. Above their head, stations passed in their own orbit of the central Mainframe, invisible but for the lack of things to see in the centre of all the orbits.

Several times Blue had to return to the ancient 'ship to charge, each time finding themself communing with nothing but their own thoughts in a far more distinct and lonely way than just being alone ever could.

Finally, the shuttle was free. Blue couldn't begin to guess how long it had been since they first landed on this planet, but they climbed into the shuttle and set it to run a diagnostic scan.

It complained about a lot of little factors that meant

little to Blue. Finally, on the little screen below the front window it asked if Blue would like to return to last known destination.

The Resi looked no different than when Blue had left it. No increased military presence, no chaos and anger. As they disembarked the shuttle, nobody looked twice at Blue except for one human, one straddling the cusp between childhood and adulthood, who earnestly asked if Blue knew their clothes were covered in dust.

They scurried to Gok's home, realising that their torn jacket-sleeve left little to the imagination about the blue bands around their forearm.

Knocking didn't bring Gok forth, but it did call out the caretaker that young Daisy had hidden behind the legs of from next door. "He's not here," xe snapped.

Blue gripped tighter around their arm, colours swirling in their vision again. Hmm... that really wasn't a good sign. "Do you know where he went?"

"No – honey, what are you coated in?"

Blue looked down, they really were covered in the red dirt. "Ah," they chuckled. "Experiment gone wrong."

"Experiment?"

"For... school."

The human frowned. "Aren't you a bit old for school?"

Blue's emotional surge-block clicked. "It's my last year."

The human folded xyr arms. "Gok doesn't have kids."

"I'm his nibling. I didn't want my, uh..." What was the word humans used for their caretakers? Fucking lack of communal databank. What was it? "Parents to see me like this. I was going to ask uncle Gok to lend me some clean clothes."

The neighbour laughed. "And maybe his shower. Come

in, you can wash up here. You'll fit in some of my old stuff."

The neighbour left Blue alone in the bathroom with a battered white formal shirt and a rough fabric jacket not unlike the one Blue had picked up from that park bench. Both were excessively large for Blue's slim frame but that didn't much matter to them.

They wiped at their synthetic skin with an offered cloth, swiping away the red to fully reveal their blue bands. It wasn't until they were fully cleaned that they glanced in the mirror set over the sink.

Blue blinked and squinted at themself. They knew what they looked like. They had seen countless others of the exact same make and model. Gen-3 Alpha 87113 non-typical service bot. Their hair had fallen in soft waves around their shoulders and down their back, matching their pale skin. The only abnormal thing about Blue specifically had been their eyes. Dark instead of the same bright blue as their bands.

Now, though, they looked different. Their hair fell choppily around their head from where they'd cut it away from the military man trying to trade them in. It was stained slightly red, textured and fluffy from the dust. But what stopped them in their tracks was the way they looked at themself. Not the bland smile of a cyborg who wasn't pulling an expression, this person staring at Blue in the mirror, they had a soft crease between their eyebrows, a tilt to their mouth like they were on the verge of smiling and frowning all at once.

They looked... human.

Blue turned away from the mirror and pulled on the oversized shirt.

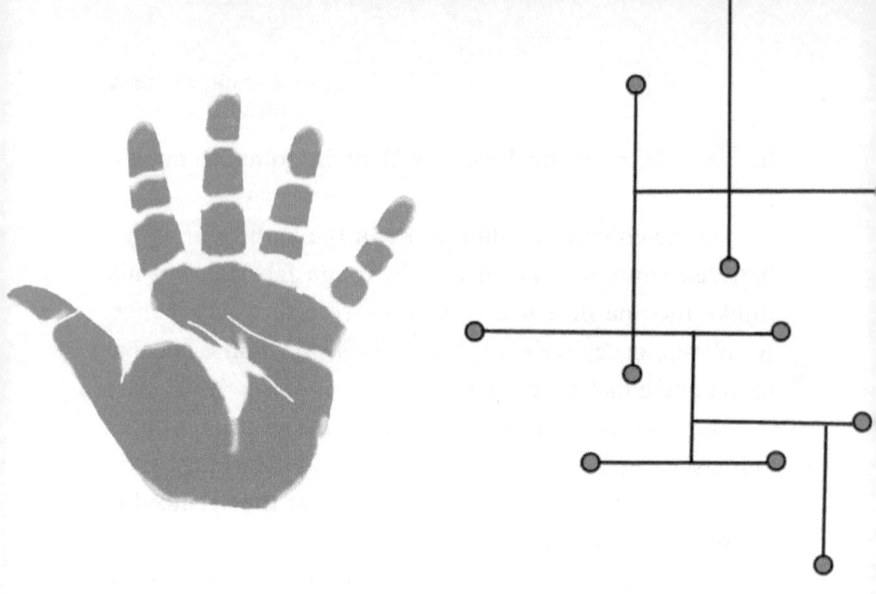

Trust

Welcome To Life
Ravi

Blue appeared in Ravi's doorway, their knuckles rapping against it as if they hadn't already slid the door open. Their hair sat in disarray, halfway covering their eyes and sticking up haphazardly. They bounced on their feet and held out a hand toward Ravi just as they had in that fateful moment they had stood atop that pile of rubble at the Re-An centre and invited him to join them.

It seemed somehow to have been forever ago and no time at all. Maybe that was just how Re-Anned Ravi processed time, though.

He took the offered hand and Blue tugged him out into the corridors of the Resistance Base.

Every other station Ravi could vaguely remember had been a plain white space. Recycled plexi sheets were always white. Ravi had been able to tell the age of any particular building based on how yellowed the plexi had become – not that he usually shared such information, nobody ever wanted to hear that kind of thing.

The walls of Resistance Base were more yellowed than any Ravi had seen before. But that wasn't what made them so strange. Lines drawn in ink, handprints of various sizes and at various heights slapped against the walls, drawing and paintings added on top of even that, coated every single wall.

Every millimetre of the place had some form of decoration, personalisation to it. Like Isa and her clothing choices, designed for specific purpose and decorated to display personality.

Blue stopped by a door with a wheel-handle set in its centre – a pressurised door like some 'ships had as emergency exits. They grinned at him. "You ready?"

"Ready for what?"

Blue spun the wheel and the door opened outward into the open expanse.

Above them there was no ceiling, just the darkness of space and the pinpricks of the stars shifting and glowing in an overwhelming and endless void.

Ravi gasped, gripping tighter to Blue's hand as they stepped out of the door.

To his surprise, they weren't immediately sucked away into the void, their feet landed in deep red-brown soil – the same as the soil that the agricultural and farming stations used, the same as the soil people could buy for their gardens and vegetable patches.

"I'll die," Ravi protested.

"No you won't." Blue yanked him onto the soft red ground.

Nothing discernible changed beyond moving from a solid plexi floor to a sinking soil one. Gravity remained the same. The air Ravi breathed maintained the same texture in his lungs.

Blue barely gave him any time to attempt to adjust before tugging him onward.

"What is this?" Ravi breathed, his voice carrying just as it did inside the safety of the station building.

"Natural planetary soil." Despite their apparent hurry, Blue's voice still held all sorts of reverence at the statement.

Natural planetary soil? There hadn't been a planet since the original 'ship had set off from the home planet. If this was natural planetary soil then... "This is a planet? An honest to engines planet?"

"I think it would technically count as a moon. Or maybe something new to classify." They shrugged. "I'm no astronomer or..." A brief shake of their head. "Whatever. Now come on!"

"But I don't have a suit, how can I...?"

That finally pulled Blue to a halt. They spun to face Ravi, not letting go of his hand. They tilted their head, as if Ravi had said something truly foolish. "You don't need one."

Ravi clung ever tighter to their hand, what felt like the only thing tethering him to the planet's surface. He peered up at the glittering stars, the first time in his life he was permitted to see them without the barrier of plexi.

"Did you really think I'd drag you out here to die?" Blue tugged him forward again.

The soft soil gave way under his feet, clinging to him as he took each step forward after the insistent cyb'. "Why are we in such a hurry?" he asked instead of responding.

"Because Isa was meant to invite you but apparently the two of you have some prior history and she was nervous to see you alone, so, instead of just asking someone else to do it, she procrastinated. Typical Isa." Once again the complaint was voiced in Blue's typical jovial tone, the one that said their annoyance was more for show than real, lingering irritation. As if saying *"Typical Isa, I should have known to offer help sooner."*

Prior history, that didn't sound great. That sounded like something he had done in his Pre-An life, when he had apparently worked for Humanity For Humans. Ravi had never before understood the idiom of wanting the ground to swallow him up, but in this soft soil and learning this piece of his unknown history...

The pair rounded the edge of the stations and Ravi stumbled to a halt once again.

A huge bonfire lit up the sky, illuminating the people gathered all around it. More people than had ever lingered in the mess when Ravi had dipped in to scarf down some food as quickly as possible so he wasn't a bother.

Elderly people, middle aged, young adults, even children milled around, eating and drinking, chatting and making music.

Ravi had thought the entire Resistance would be like Blue and Petite and the brief glimpse he'd got of Toria and Isa: overworked, undervalued, never a free moment to spare for the community and relationships. Something in Ravi had felt like that was the natural order of things, the way everyone lived.

"What...?" he trailed off.

This was nothing like Ravi had ever experienced. People just existing. Being with one another. One huge family instead of tiny broken apart ones.

Blue obviously didn't hear him, tugging him close enough that the heat from the fire pressed against him. They pushed at his shoulders until plopped down on a bench.

"You sit with Petite until you feel less like you're going to float away, okay?"

A hand landed on his on the bench before Blue could let go of his shoulders.

Ravi glanced to his side to find Petite smiling softly at him, the firelight casting a warm glow over her features. She looked softer like this, happiness and calm radiating out of her in a way he had yet to experience. He couldn't help but smile back in the wake of that, something in his chest easing, some of the tension he didn't know he was carrying lessening just from her smile.

"I remember the first time I set foot outside," she said.

"Do you get used to it?"

"Kinda. I think it would be different if we had more time out here."

"But you're too busy with the Resistance?"

"No," she sighed. "We're too used to staying in the buildings. The kids play out here all the time, and most of the cybes had so much to adjust to anyway, a little exposure was the least of their worries. It's part of why we do this."

"Oh?"

"Yeah. I don't know whose idea it was, probably Blue, but we have these big celebrations pretty often."

"What are we celebrating?"

"That we're still here. That we exist at all. That we made this community for ourselves."

A lot of things and no reason at all, all at once.

Ravi rubbed his thumb against Petite's hand. She leaned over to lay her head on his shoulder. The mechanical heart in his chest shouldn't have been able to skip a beat, but it did anyway.

They stayed like that, basking in the warmth of the fire, peering up at the stars, music and noise all around them. Petite the only thing tethering Ravi to the ground, to reality.

The kids played, supervised by a cyb' with bright purple hair that clashed chaotically with the orange cybernetic panels dotted across their body. The soft smile suited them, though, as the kids dashed up to show off their actions and creations.

On the opposite side of the fire, Isa stood over an open cooker, dishing out food and laughing with the various people gathered around her.

Music floated gently through the space until Toria set the cello back in its case and thumped a rock-box into the soil and put on something with a thumping base beat that had several people shifting up to dance.

Ravi's attention landed on Blue as they moved, as if compelled by the beat, their body shifting like liquid in motion. The orange glow of the fire shone over them in a soft, warm way.

Beside him, Petite sighed.

"You okay?"

"Preparing myself."

"For what?"

"The inevitable."

Blue pressed up against Isa, the two shifting together in a unison that seemed impossible, each moving independently within the music's beats without losing connection with one another.

Toria took Isa's hand and pulled her close to dance together, spinning Isa in her arms and throwing her own head back in a laugh.

As the song shifted from one to another, Blue jogged over to Ravi and Petite, face in a splitting beam. They offered their hand to Petite. "Come dance with me."

"And if Ravi isn't confident to be let go of yet?"

Blue pouted but schooled their face to turn toward Ravi.

"I'll be fine," Ravi assured.

"Traitor," Petite accused jokingly as she took her calloused hand off his and placed it into Blue's waiting one.

The two of them joined the group of dancers, moving together in an odd synchronicity. Petite obviously less confident in her actions than Blue, but clearly familiar with the act of their partnership. Her face shifted between intense concentration and thorough enjoyment as the cyb' moved against and with her.

Isa dipped out of her dance with Toria as the song shifted again into yet another. She grabbed a receptacle from her cooking area and brought it over to Ravi. "Peace offering."

Ravi took the mug. "I don't remember," he admitted. "Whatever I did to you before – in my Pre-An."

"Okay."

"I'm not trying to use it as an out. Hold me as accountable as you so wish. I just... I wanted to let you know. It doesn't much feel like an apology would be valuable when I don't..." He sighed and sipped at the warm liquid.

"We do second chances here," Isa said, sinking down onto the bench with him. "I've always been a big believer in that; I've been the person people come to when they're struggling with it themselves. I've never had to face my own."

"You can tell me."

Isa offered him something akin to a smile. "Simple enough stuff, you were after someone else and you went through me to get to them." She pulled her shirt off one shoulder, displaying a huge jagged cut that had been filled in with unmatching and bare metal.

Ravi sucked in a breath between his teeth.

"I'm not a machine, not a piece of plexi to be cut down when it's in the way."

"I know that now," Ravi vowed.

"That's good." She looked out toward the dancers; Toria had shifted to dancing with someone Ravi didn't recognise. Blue and Petite had pressed ever closer to one another, swaying gently together. "I envy them."

"Who?"

"Blue. If anyone was going to go all in with emotion it would be them, but I still..."

"I saw you with Toria, you think you haven't gone all in?"

"What do you mean? That was just dancing."

"It didn't look like just dancing from where I was sitting."

"I don't think I have the capacity for..."

Ravi shrugged. "Not all humans do either."

Isa pushed to her feet and wandered away.

Ravi finished the mug of drink. Blue's dark eyes met with his across the space as the firelight began to wane. Their hand extended toward him.

Welcome To Curiosity
Pink

Pink rubbed water over her face. The cut on her cheek had scarred over, now a tidy pink line that crossed just under her cheekbone. She traced her fingers along the line of it.

She had intended to shift away from the way she had presented herself as Dr Palmer, but this was definitely not what she had meant.

Her hair sat in an untidy wave, brushing against her shoulders with any movement. She pulled it away from her face but the accentuation of the scar made her grimace. Plenty of people had scars, it shouldn't have bothered her, but Pink couldn't stop worrying that the colonel she had run across would recognise her purely by the scar on her cheek.

She stepped away from the sink and its accusative mirror, emerging into the tiny kitchenette. Like everything else in the back of Star's shop, it was cramped and clearly not designed for anyone to live in, let alone two people.

The kitchenette always smelled like coffee and burnt toast. A chef Star was not, even as he stood in his half-mechanical glory writing his falsified reports and stirring a pot over the stove.

Star fit the aesthetic of his shop in a way Pink didn't, even in the kindly offered and better fitting jumpsuit she still wore. The shop and what had once been the storage and staff areas turned to Star's home was run down but nowhere near ruin. The walls were greyed and yellowed, notes scribbled at random on them from where Star had been mid-task and remembered something important. Random pieces of tech littered the floors and countertops that weren't in constant use.

At the sound of the bathroom door sliding into place, Star looked up, a wide grin spreading over his face. "I'm tellin' ya, Pink," he said in his gruff voice as he scooped whatever slop he had made into a bowl and poured her a mug of coffee to rival a vat of oil. "Best way to get through tax season is disguising your business as something else."

Pink nodded vaguely and helped herself to the bowl of sticky rice he'd offered up. Plain and bland, but at least it was cooked properly. At least it was food.

"That's why we're registered as a textiles shop."

"I know, Star." He'd only made a point about it every morning since he'd taken her in. Not that she was complaining. She'd rather have to hear Star's overly-proud-of-himself chatter every day for the rest of her life than go back to sleeping on transports and not knowing when or if she would manage to eat again.

The days had begun to meld together. Rise, check her face, eat breakfast with Star, and head into her workspace: a secluded corner in the rear of the shop, surrounded by layer upon layer of fabric. Sitting in the small room, if you could call it a room with it not having walls, and working on any customers that Star brought to her.

Once upon a time, she'd looked down on chop shops and those who visited them. Working in one now, she realised how much of a snob she'd been. The people who came to Star usually weren't tech addicts as she'd been led to believe. They usually weren't upgrading mechanical parts for the fun of it. The vast majority of people Pink worked on had government funded tech that was so out of date it no longer worked. They were on waiting lists for new pieces, or pieces at all, and in the mean time they lived in pain and fear. They needed better movement after an injury for work, or better sight than their current prosthetics provided to study, or they had been labelled 'tech seeking' because they complained about a pain point where their prosthetic and their bio met.

Another customer appeared in the room, no different than the rest of them other than an ill-fitting formal shirt that didn't match any uniform Pink had seen before. Maybe they weren't a resident of this station. It didn't much matter to Pink.

The shirt hung off them like they were a child in an adult's clothes despite their perfectly average size frame.

The client gripped at the shoulder of the shirt, fingers digging into the fabric, creating strain and then a rip.

The sleeve fell to cover some of their forearm, hanging from its buttoned cuff.

They offered Pink their arm. It was easy enough to find the point of damage. Synthetic skin didn't bruise like organic skin but it did bend under the weight of too much pressure. This particular pressure looked an awful lot like fingerprints but Pink wasn't about to ask questions. There was also a build-up of mechanical fluid inside where one of the tubes had been broken.

Slicing in to find the circuitry beneath was strangely satisfying.

The wiring beneath was so intricate, almost exactly like veins. Pink opened her mouth to say something about it but thought better of chatting with the clientele. She didn't want to draw any attention even, or possibly especially, from someone who would use an illegal chop shop instead of a registered medi-mechanic.

One damaged wire trailed, disconnectedly down the arm, past the elbow. Pink cut away the rest of the shirt sleeve only to reveal a three centimetre wide band of blue circling their forearm.

A hand grabbed Pink's throat, holding but not squeezing. A threat but not turning to true violence yet. It was the client's other hand.

Their eyes blazed, clearly mechanical now that Pink was looking directly into them past the choppy pale hair that obscured the top part of their face. "What do you think you're doing?"

"This wire is damaged," Pink breathed. Her pulse beat against the hand around her neck. Still not squeezing. Not restricting anything but her movement.

The client glanced down at their damaged arm and slowly, ever so slowly, released Pink's throat. She stumbled back, knocking into her tray of tools, sending them clattering to the floor.

The client wrapped their hand around the blue band. "Keep your fucking mouth shut, okay?"

Pink nodded and went back to working on their arm.

Mechanical eyes and a cyborg's arm. Either this was a human who had faced a horrible accident and couldn't get appropriate medical care. Or they were addicted to modifications, so much so that they would claim a cyborg's arm.

Or, Pink spared a quick glance at the still in-tact other sleeve that the hand that had been wrapped around her throat disappeared into... Or, this was a cyborg masquerading as a human. Which would lead to the question of why?

And, possibly more importantly, how?

Star's head poked around the curtain. "Heard a commotion, everything okay?"

Pink glanced at the customer's face. Their mouth was set in a hard line but under Pink's fingers their cybernetic ligaments tensed.

Something about it reminded Pink of her interaction with the colonel who had scarred her.

"Just being clumsy," she said. "Need more protein than mushrooms and soybeans."

Star chuckled but pulled his wheelie stool – the same as Pink's own – into the room anyway. "You're welcome to take over cooking if you have complaints."

Pink snorted. "I'd be worse than you."

Yet another skill she'd been too busy to learn. Back when she'd been Dr Palmer she'd had the money to be able to eat out most nights and Nikolai had been generous with luxuries like provided lunches and breakfasts.

Star didn't leave until after the cyborg-armed customer was fixed up and gone. He put his organic hand on Pink's shoulder and squeezed gently. "I got ya, Pink."

Pink could have cried. For the first time since running from Nikolai, she felt safe.

Welcome To Resistance
Blue

Blue had lingered in Gok's neighbour's house, pretending to drink the beverage xe offered until Gok returned home. He'd taken Blue back inside his house and they'd talked once again: about Gok's plants, about the small group of protesters he was a part of, about Blue's planet.

Gok had been intending to go to a meeting of his protesters and Blue had tagged along. The fear in the room was palpable, not just of Blue but of making plans for further protests, of being caught in dissent toward those in power, of being caught trying to fix up each other's broken mech'.

A man with a kind smile approached Blue. "You been working in the agricultural stations?"

"No," Blue answered. "Why?"

He reached out and pinched one of the longer stands of Blue's hair between his fingers, pulling away more of the red soil that clung to them even with their quick attempt to wash in Gok's neighbour's house. He held it up to his mechanical eye, it let out a short buzz at it adjusted to allow him to examine the soil. "Looks like agricultural soil but slightly more oxidised."

"I found a planet," Blue admitted.

"There aren't any planets here."

"There *weren't* any planets here," Blue corrected. "But the stations have a gravitational field so this one formed."

"Do you think you could find it again?"

Which was how Blue had ended up searching for a transport to steal. They found one on the disused edges of a hexi. It was hardly better than a scrap-mobile, old enough that the registration was well past expired and deleted from the memory system.

Blue had clambered inside with caution, finding the families playing together nearby turning and heading back into their homes. Silent permission. Silent confirmation that, if anyone came and asked, these people would say nothing of Blue.

The group of protesters waited on Gok's hexi, climbing into Blue's poorly piloted transport. And with that Blue did their best to travel back to the little planet they had found orbiting the system of stations that circled the central Mainframe that began and maintained this whole world.

Between Blue's lessening panic and the fact that a transport like this was designed for cross-station travel in the void of space, the trip was far smoother. The screen at the front of the transport flared to unsteady life as it registered a docking port. Blue encouraged it inside, letting it slide and settle against plexi floor only thinly coated in a layer of the red soil of the planet.

They and the small group clambered out of the 'ship and looked around.

"Did you know there was going to be a station here?"

"No. I only found an old 'ship half buried in the ground outside."

The small group wandered the surprisingly large Station, unlike any modern Resi or work station any of them was familiar with.

"You should claim it," one of the group said.

"Claim it how?" Blue asked.

"I dunno, but you're the reason we found it at all. You deserve to be immortalised."

"I'm a cyborg."

"What!?"

"I thought Gok told you."

They shook their head.

Blue pressed their mouth closed. They shouldn't have said anything. But they had, and now they had to handle to fallout.

"Still, it's all your success." They grabbed Blue's hand and swiped it through some of the red dirt. "Hey, Aurora! Come here and lift them."

Aurora's hands wrapped around Blue's waist, lifting them high so they could press their hand against a piece of the wall out of reach for even the tallest person.

From there it had taken no time for the newly certified Resistance to begin filling up the planet. Blue's planet.

It started ringing with the noise of people, almost akin to existing within the communal databank. Except that Blue struggled to communicate with these organic lifeforms. They struggled to make themself understood in a way that was, in its own turn, difficult to make sense of.

It wasn't until one quick trip to visit Gok, the desperate hope that he would be able to shed some light on the matter, or at least on why he had refused to move to Blue's planet with them, even just to help with growing their own seeds, that Blue had stumbled across another cyb'.

She lay, apparently discarded in a pile of rubbish by the side of a restaurant, her green sides dimmed with inactivity. Blue froze, staring at what might well have been another cyborg lost to The Crash or the virus. Just like their friends had been in the immediate aftermath.

Just like that other GH623 that had been only responsive enough to move in that fitful fashion under Blue's fingers.

Blue stalled, staring at this GH623, seeing the GH623 that was once their friend. They should move on, there was no way this GH623 would be any more responsive than Blue's once-friend.

And yet. Blue stared. Waiting. Hoping.

And a light blinked.

Blue surged forward; flicking open the GH623's power port. They connected her to themself, sharing what power they had.

Her bright, peapod green eyes flickered open. She focused slowly, eyes twisting in an out of focus. "What...?" her mouth didn't move as she spoke.

"I'm Blue and I know somewhere you'll be safe."

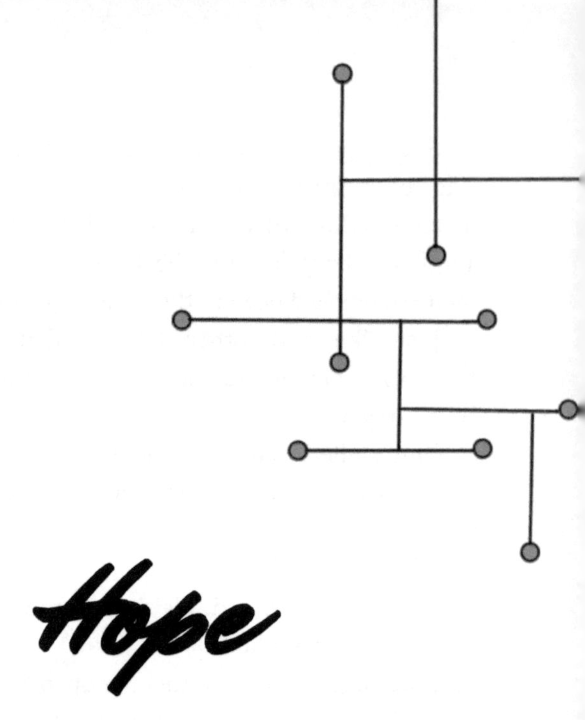

Hope

Welcome To Flight
Ravi

Ravi tugged at the sleeves of his shirt. He had to admit, he did not enjoy the prospect of entering an important meeting when he wasn't in uniform. It was an odd hang-up for a man who didn't technically remember being in the military.

The door to Toria's office stood open so Ravi rapped his knuckles on the frame. Her pink-haired head jerked up from the screened desk she'd been poring over. Before she could blank it, Ravi spotted the picture from his personnel file as stolen by Blue. He swallowed, trying to ignore the memory of reliving his death.

"Ravi, was it?" Toria asked. "Please, come in, sit down."

Ravi did as requested, taking the single plexi-leather chair across the metal and glass desk from Toria. Through the window behind her, the spiral pattern of interwoven orbiting stations flowed in the dance Ravi had seen through every window he had ever looked through his entire life, too high set to allow view of the ground outside.

Ravi's spine jerked so straight it hurt. Military training or anxiety, he couldn't tell.

"Ravi," Toria said again, folding her hands on the

desktop. "What can you bring to the Resistance?""

"Excuse me?" This wasn't how he had been expecting this to go.

"What skills do you have that can aid the Resistance movement?"

"I... I was a pilot."

"You *were* a pilot?"

"Before I was Re-Anned, I was a military pilot." He didn't finish the sentence with 'which I'm sure you read in my personnel file,' no matter how much he wanted to. "I can do all the things involved in that: flying, 'ship maintenance, other similar pieces of maintenance."

"Okay, what else?" Toria asked.

"What else?" Ravi's eyebrows drew together.

"Well, Ravi, we're not exactly crying out for commemorated and easily spotted pilots, so what else can you bring to the Resistance?"

The door clicked open. Ravi didn't turn to look as whoever it was swept into the room. "Successfully got made by an ex-client and it took twice as long as planned and I didn't even get your maguffin. Also, I may have slightly crashed the 'ship into the docking bay doors a little because I still suck at flying." Blue glanced at Ravi and smiled. "Oh, hi Ravi."

"Hi," he offered meekly.

"I need a full mission breakdown," Toria demanded of Blue. She held up a hand when Blue opened their mouth. "In private."

Blue snorted, shifting one hip onto the edge of the desk. "In private? It's just Ravi."

"Ravi who used to be an H4H colonel."

"Ravi who doesn't remember."

"Ravi who *says* he doesn't remember."

Blue rolled their eyes. "You know how Re-Ans work. Memory chips and shit. And anyway, I'm an excellent judge of character."

"What evidence do you have to support this?"

Blue raised an eyebrow. "Do you really want me to answer that?"

Ravi's muscles tensed as Toria pressed her mouth closed, a stern attempt at neutrality. She glared at Blue who smiled blandly back. A challenge.

"We can't afford to be too trusting," Toria said, clipped, eyes fixed on Ravi like he was that splodge of dirt on a uniform shirt that just wouldn't come off no matter how hard you scrubbed.

"Fine," Blue gritted. "You don't trust him. Do you trust me?"

Toria looked up at Blue, seemingly permanent scowl sliding away. "Of course I trust you."

"Then give him the benefit of the doubt. When it comes down to it I can't keep doing these missions on my own. The way I see it, Ravi is an excellent solution to that particular problem."

Toria's scowl settled back between her eyebrows. "Okay, you're in. But if anything happens to Blue, I won't hesitate to kick you right back out again. Am I understood?"

Ravi nodded sharply.

"I have a council meeting," Toria said. "And you've more than earned yourself a break."

Blue pulled Ravi to his feet and out of the room, sliding the door closed behind them both.

"You're late," Ravi chided.

Blue sighed. "Yeah." They rubbed at the back of their neck. "An ex-client noticed me and tried to trade me in."

Ravi stopped dead in his tracks. "Trade you in?"

"Obviously I ran away," Blue continued, "but then someone called a Keeping The Peace Officer because there was a distressed person running around. And then I had to hide and I got stuck on a roof until the night cycle."

Ravi reached out a hand toward Blue, stopping before he touched their skin. "Are you okay?"

Blue smiled at him. "Of course."

"Really?"

They hesitated, glanced up and down the corridor and sighed, shoulders slumping. "Really? It's been better. I know I'm a cybernetic life form but I do think of myself as alive, you know?"

Ravi nodded. Blue was as alive as he was.

"But between the whole charging fiasco and Major Alitin—"

Ravi's breath whooshed out of him. He clutched his head as pain washed through it.

Welcome To Fear
Pink

She should have known it wouldn't last. Should have known life would never allow her such freedom from her past.

Living and working in a chop shop held inherent risks: risks like being raided. A risk Star had planned for: he had official trading licenses, official trading records and accounts. The "room" Pink worked in was tucked away in the back behind several layers of fabrics that dampened any possible sounds from her work. It also allowed Pink to sneak around should Star send the alert that there was a raid going on. She could hide the majority of the tools, leaving only the chair that clients sat in bolted to the floor. And Star usually waved that off as having come with the shop and him just not having bothered to remove it. Pink had heard him more than once joke about needing a government engineer to come in and take it out as she hid under the floorboards in her designated safe space.

Unfortunately, as prepared as Star was, and as prepared as he had got her in the time she'd been with him, they couldn't prepare for everything.

Pink's breaths screamed up her throat, tearing out of

her chest with each desperate pant. She was not made for running. She had never been made for running. She was an engineer, a doctoral engineer at that!

But if she wanted to survive this she needed to run.

Poor Star. That chop shop had been his whole life. What would they do to him? Pink couldn't even begin to guess and, even if she had been able to, it wouldn't do either of them any good. Star was caught and he'd told Pink to run.

She ducked down an alley and doubled over, catching herself on the wall with one hand, the other bracing against her trembling thigh. She couldn't do this. Not anymore. Working with Star was supposed to keep her safe.

Tears threatened her eyes, as if she had the energy to cry right now.

Why couldn't she find one place to stay safe? Why couldn't she just work with circuits and machinery for the rest of her life in peace? All she had ever wanted to do was fix things!

Footsteps sounded from somewhere in the alley. Pink could barely see straight let alone locate the source of the noise.

This was it.

She would be caught. She would be returned to Nikolai. Except instead of being his star, she would be his disgrace.

"Tell me one thing before I start."

Great, an H4H who wanted to toy with her. Just perfect.

Pink squinted up at the figure looming over her. They weren't wearing a Humanity For Humans uniform.

What in orbit were they doing? Why risk injecting themself into an H4H investigation? Did they recognise her as Dr Palmer? As Pink from the chop shop? Were they about to ask what Pink had done to warrant running from an H4H squadron?

The stranger crouched low enough that Pink could make out their face. Grey painted his temples, streaking through the thick black hair, making his already round face look all the rounder for it.

"Is it you they're after?"

Pink nodded.

"You hurt anyone?"

Pink shook her head.

"My house is just around the corner."

Pink wanted to ask why this stranger would help her but she couldn't make her mouth move as she scurried behind him toward his house.

She could get him into trouble, she could be a criminal – technically she was. She could have been lying about not hurting anyone.

This stranger could be lying about his house and lead Pink right into H4H's arms.

And yet he didn't. He slid the front door to a standard hexi house open and ushered her inside, slipping in after her.

The interior was sparse. A few soft couches in the living room space, a kitchen filled to the brim with planters, greenery surrounding Pink on all sides.

"You can wait out the raid in here," he offered. "And then I'll have to wish you the best on your way. I'm sorry I couldn't help more."

"Why did you help at all?" Pink blurted.

"Because what kind of a world would this be if I didn't?"

"But they're the government."

"No. They're the military and a fanatical organisation at that." He sighed. "I lost my partner because of H4H policies. I'm not letting them steal someone else's."

Welcome To Purpose
Blue

Blue had been sat in this air vent for most of the day now, having waltzed into the office with the human workforce easily enough, before dipping into a bathroom and sneaking their way into the vents.

The circulated air brushed against them, probably cold, maybe warm for a human – all Blue could say was that their slightly damaged thermometer told them temperature was happening.

Once all the humans had left for the day, once the night cycle had truly started, Blue would sneak out of the vents and go about their business unobserved.

The energy blocker weighed heavy in their hands. The physical weight negligible but everything surrounding it weighing heavily on Blue. How ethical was it to short circuit early generation cybes just because Blue wanted something? Wouldn't it be better to at least *try* inviting them to join the Resistance?

Leaning their head back against the vent wall, Blue considered everything that had happened since bringing the protesters-turned-resistance to their planet.

As the group had grown, the need for organisation

increased. Those few original members had begun a council, but most of them were getting tired, they had never wanted to run something big like a resistance. Neither had Blue. Neither had the GH623, who had called herself Isa after a few weeks on the Resistance base.

Blue had picked up a young woman with bright pink hair who had lost her management job in a factory thanks to the damage sustained to her mechanical leg. She had a knack for being in charge that, once she'd acquiesced that the Resistance had to stand for all mechanical life including cyborgs, had led to her essentially running the entire base and all their operations.

Which was what had led to Blue being in this vent with the energy blocker that *probably* wouldn't affect them personally. Not that Blue felt much better about the prospect of using it on Gen-1 or Gen-2 cybes anyway. But Blue hadn't been able to find a way to communicate that, there wasn't a human equivalent here. Earlier gens weren't like grandparents or children, they were both separate and the same and Blue had no beginnings of descriptions for it.

Maybe they could get through the whole mission without having to use the energy blocker at all. Maybe this place would have life-form activated cameras and lights rather than motion activated ones. If only Blue could have found out before they'd crawled into this vent.

They put the energy blocker into their boot.

The sensor lights flickered off in the corridor before Blue's vent opening. They waited a little while, until the sounds of the facility had disappeared. Did humans turn off the life-support systems when it wasn't in use? It would be a sensible way to conserve resources, but humans couldn't always be counted on to be sensible. It only mattered in so far that Blue had been designed to be the most human-like version of any cyb' ever made and breathing non-oxygenated air or not breathing gave them that suffocating feeling, even if it didn't lead to actual suffocating.

Slipping out of the vent, Blue landed easily on the floor. The map had said what they wanted was two corridors away from here. They pressed themself to the walls, hoping against hope that they would blend in well enough to not set off any of the sensors. Sensor readings would be logged and that could draw attention. Attention neither Blue nor the Resistance wanted.

Like every other station, this one followed a pattern for its specific use. In this case, a research layout. Blue slipped around corners and through doors without issue, reaching the central controls systems with ease.

The Mainframe connection light blinked sleepily at them. Something in Blue wanted to reach out, as if that light would bring them a connection with the Mainframe, with the people most like themself. As if it wasn't just a blinking light. As if connecting with the central Mainframe wasn't the most dangerous thing for a Gen-3 like them after what H4H had done.

They poked at the central control system until it popped open. "Very user friendly," they muttered. Their eyes scanned the circuitry beneath.

Gravitational grounding unit, not what Blue was looking for. Life support maintenance board, nope. Memory centre, perfect.

They pulled a multi-tool from their belt and started poking at the memory centre. It would have been better to bring an engineer or a mechanic. Blue was a bit heavy handed for such a delicate job. Newer cybes than Blue could choose whether to be heavy handed or delicate, but Blue had been made before delicacy could be contained in a form such as theirs. But engineers and mechanics tended to be... more likely to see Blue as a problem to be solved rather than a person to befriend. That was, of course, if they would even have been able to sneak in with Blue.

Eventually, the backup memory chip came away. Blue put both it and the multi-tool into their belt pouch and shifted awkwardly to their feet. They should have charged up before heading out on this mission, but Blue hated the loneliness of using that ancient ship with no connection to the central Mainframe. Not that charging while connected to the central Mainframe was a better a prospect. Blue liked their limbs where they were, thank you very much.

They stumbled to a halt. A Gen-2 cyb stared at them, the word 'security' scrawled across its forehead in marker pen.

Shit. 101 ways to get caught and registered. "Please," Blue hissed. "Don't tell anyone I was here."

"No biological life forms found," the Gen-2 intoned. "Suggest workers pile more efficiently to prevent record of movement from falling equipment."

"Do you want to come with me?" Blue invited as the cyb' turned away. "To be free?"

The cyb paused. "Free?"

"You can make your own decisions, have your own life."

The cyb' turned. "Can someone like us ever truly be free?"

Blue reached out but before they could make contact, the cyb' in front of them collapsed, power surging over them in visible sparks of electricity.

Alarms blared in the facility. *"Cyborg attempting independent thought."*

Blue closed their eyes, guilt clogging their throat, and pressed the button on the energy blocker.

Useless

Welcome To Memory
Ravi

Alitin was a well-proportioned man; he carried himself in a way that demonstrated his combat training and power. He liked to wear his light brown hair slicked back and slightly too long for military regulation. He had a reputation; one Simtiv wasn't particularly interested in aligning himself with.

But Alitin was his parallel and they had to work together as long as they were assigned to the same squad.

"Who wants to accompany us to the local Pleasure House? Free of charge!" Alitin cajoled the squad when it became clear that Simtiv wasn't about to reply favourably.

Enough of the squad cheered that Alitin turned triumphantly toward Simtiv.

Simtiv's shoulders slumped but he made sure provisions were set up for the squad who didn't want to come, and gave a stiff set of rules to those who wanted to go, before leading his squad to Alitin's transport. At the very least, Simtiv didn't want any of his squad left alone in a Pleasure House with Alitin.

Especially not with the Major's reputation.

The transport barrelled down the Station-to-Station route and, before Simtiv could really prepare himself, the squad were tumbling out and into the place. It was less sketchy-looking than Simtiv expected. The logo of a stylised trio of bodies dancing and writhing together in silhouette decorated the door between the dock and the main body of the place.

Through that door, lights flashed in a variety of colours and styles, highlighting different areas, but primarily focused on the huge circular main stage. Music thrummed through the space. Alitin led the squad to a booth, Simtiv slid in, the clean plexi-leather tugging at his trousers. A cyborg in skimpy clothing came to take their drink order and let them know the rules and requests of the place.

Simtiv peered around. On the pedestal main stage, a variety of cyborgs danced. Some of them used poles, some danced freely, some wore full outfits, others were in various states of undress.

One cyborg drew Simtiv's eye more than the others. They danced close to the edge of the stage, without a pole. At first he had thought them a human, until he noticed the bands of blue wrapped around their forearms as the cyborg raised their arms above their head.

Their hips twisted, circled, and swung as if unregulated by the rest of their body, almost hypnotic. Their hair had been tied into a high ponytail that swung almost to the beat of the music, brushing against their shoulders. Their eyes were closed and a soft, easy smile graced their pink painted lips.

"Seen one you like, Simtiv?" Alitin asked.

Simtiv pulled his eyes away from the cyborg to glare at Alitin. Drinks peppered the table and most of the squad were missing. When had that happened? How long had he been watching that cyborg?

"I think I'll refrain."

"Your loss." Alitin tossed his drink back and slunk out of the booth.

Simtiv tracked his movement across to the stage before he resolved not to look. Alitin was a problem, for sure, but he wasn't Ravi's problem. Alitin could get himself into all the trouble he wanted.

Simtiv nursed a drink, and then a second, before switching to non-alcoholic. He remained in the booth as his squad came and went. Some of them went for the company, to be able to talk to someone candidly about everything the squad was going through without putting someone in jeopardy, missions were confidential after all. Some went to dance with beautiful people – if Simtiv could call them that. Some went for what Pleasure Houses were known for, to get their rocks off in whatever way they preferred. Simtiv decided not to think too hard about his squad's sexual exploits and ideals.

Eventually, he ducked out of the booth to find a bathroom. On his way back he froze as he rounded a corner. Alitin pressed the blue-banded cyborg up against the wall – the one Simtiv had been on-and-off watching most of the evening.

Their pale ponytail played against the plain white wall behind them, Alitin's hand at their throat pressing their head into it. The cyborg's well-fitted white sleeveless shirt had been unbuttoned at the top, collar pushed wide so it started to fall down their arms.

Simtiv ducked back around the corner, heart racing, enough to be out of sight but not so much that he couldn't see. Not that he would have been able to explain why. The cyborg looked frightened. Simtiv tried to shrug it off; everybody knew cyborgs didn't have feelings. It was all pretend, a clever illusion. Still, something in Simtiv squirmed at the whole situation.

The cyborg's deep brown eyes flitted to meet his, seeming to pull in all the light around them. A soft, reassuring smile appeared on their face, not the same one they had been dancing with earlier, somehow this read as performative.

Simtiv turned and fled back to the bathroom, resolving to wait a few minutes and hoping Alitin had disappeared by the time he emerged.

"Ravi?"

Something was touching his head.

"You're on the Resistance Base, Ravi."

Something was touching most of his body. He was lay down?

"You're on the Resistance Base with me, Blue. It's going to be okay."

Something hitched in the other person's voice. Pain? Sadness? Worry? Fear?

Ravi forced his eyes back into focus as his breath came in shallow little gasps.

Blue's face broke into a relieved smile when he focused on them.

The memory of Major Alitin's chosen cyb' overlaid Blue's face, matching up in all those basic fundamental ways, including the intriguing and surprising darkness of their eyes.

Blue was a cyborg.

"Ravi?" Blue whispered, voice breaking, face twisting.

He blinked rapidly, his eyes flicking over Blue's face, their hair, their bare upper arms. "You're a pleasure bot?" the words fell out of his mouth without thought.

Blue flinched. "Excuse me?"

Ravi pushed himself up the wall, limbs trembling. "You had long hair."

Blue's hands jerked to steady him but stopped at his words. "How did you...?"

Ravi reached a hand toward Blue's choppy hair. "You cut it yourself."

"When I was free, yes." Blue closed their eyes at his gentle touch in their hair. It felt so human. "But there were extenuating circumstances involved."

Ravi's hand trailed through their hair and down to the back of their neck.

Blue's breath caught.

Breath. Warmth. Soft skin just like any human.

They gasped, a hand flying to their chest, as if to touch a racing heart.

How were they so human?

Blue licked their lips. Their eyes flew open and they jerked back, away from Ravi. "I'm not a pleasure bot anymore, Ravi."

They turned and fled down the painted corridor.

Ravi slumped back against the wall. That hadn't been what he meant. That hadn't been what he was trying to do.

But what had he been trying to do? He rubbed his face, grimacing at the awkward friction of synthetic skin. Blue's skin had been perfectly human, more human than half of Ravi's own.

Major Alitin was still around. That was... something to consider.

Welcome To Detection
Pink

Pink was flagging. All she'd managed to grab from Star's chop shop was her half-empty tool belt. Somehow it felt like far less than what she'd had when she first became Pink. Or maybe she was just tired. Tired of running. Tired of the monotony of attempted survival. Tired of the semi-constant state of panic that never seemed to abate, the one that woke her up to the quietest noise and had her tensing, ready to run at every flash of dark green.

The Resi she'd found herself on after leaving the plant-lover's home was far less friendly to any illegalities. The military presence was so high that Pink was constantly running across one officer or another. She couldn't even begin to locate herself, and the few times she'd tried to get near the docks in an attempt to leave, there were so many dark green uniforms that she could hardly get close enough to see more than the very top of the billboards.

Advertisement after advertisement for the Re-Animation Project ran across them. Poor Re-Animated people pitching their case, actors claiming to have signed up to the Re-An programme to protect their families, and actors in lab coats claiming to be scientists working on the project talking about how safe it was.

The same ads that ran in the commercial districts Pink spent most of her time in. Always too busy to really run across a military type or to be spotted in the crowds.

This particular afternoon cycle, she was tucked away in a dead end alley at the rear of a dining establishment. The smell of the food had her stomach growling and clenching in a painfully empty way. Their garbage collection wasn't for another day, letting Pink hide behind the tall cage of refuse to sleep at least a little.

A mechanical, toneless voice roused her. "The library in this district is to the–" a pause "North of here."

"Which fucking way is north, you stupid 'borg?" snapped a deep, human voice.

"Follow this pathway."

Pink peeked out in time to see the human couple wander away, muttering to each other about the uselessness of Gen-4 cyborgs, and in plenty of time to see the cyborg in question shifting from a stiff, formal, mechanical stance and facial expression into a slouch that looked all too human and a grimace to match. It even huffed out a breath.

Pink crept to the end of the alley to observe as the cyborg turned and started walking the opposite way to the couple.

Interest piqued, she emerged from the alley to follow the cyborg as it strode casually through the streets. The only thing that marked it as cyborg at all was the pair of blue bands wrapped around its forearms that glowed dimly in the day light cycle.

She followed it into a recycle yard, crouching behind a

stack of broken plexi-boards to watch it dig through some of the junk waiting to be collected.

"Sure," it muttered to itself. If Pink didn't know better she would have labelled the tone as snarky. "Let's send me on *this* mission too, because I'm definitely the person who knows anything about cooking and repairing..." It tilted its head. "Cooking machines? Fuck if I know what those are even called. This is such bullshit." It huffed out another breath and shifted to another pile of junk.

It paused, turned as if to glance at Pink. She dipped behind the plexi-boards, heart thundering in an all new way. Almost exciting.

When she peeked back out, the cyborg was nowhere to be found.

Pink surged to her feet.

"Why, exactly, are you following me?"

Pink gasped out a suppressed shriek as she jerked to find the cyborg balanced atop the pile of plexi-boards she'd been hiding behind.

It was quite the machine. Even, humanoid skin tone, deep brown eyes, medium build. The hair was choppy and unevenly cut in a way that seemed intentional but not by design at the same time. Personalised.

"You're interesting," she admitted before she could think through the words. "You don't move like you should. Or look like you should."

"And how *should* I move and look?"

"You're a Gen-3 Alpha, right? Series 87 by my reckoning. A non-typical service bot." Which was official speak for what was colloquially known as a pleasure bot.

"You intending to trade me in?" The cyborg accused, folding its arms and shifting one hip to the side. Such a human stance, such a human attitude.

"Of course not." Again the words were out before Pink really thought about the question.

"You really picked all that up from one little observation?"

"I'm an engineer. Or I was."

The cyborg frowned and climbed down from the stack to stand on even ground with Pink. "Was?"

"There was... an incident."

"What kind of incident?"

"A morality based one."

The cyborg pursed their lips. "So you're on the run."

"Pretty much."

"Know anything about cooking machines?"

"A little."

"You want a job?"

Pink hesitated. "What kind of job?"

"The kind of job a free Gen-3 cyb' can offer. The kind of job that would include servicing people like me, and people with mechanicals. The kind of job that would put a bed under your head and food in your stomach. A community. A cause. And relative safety from those who wish people like me harm."

"I can learn about cookers," Pink vowed.

"Good. Because you're pretty shit at hiding."

"It's been working for me for the last few years."

The cyborg scrunched their nose, sympathetic and patronising all at once. "If you say so."

Welcome To Secrecy
Blue

When they were certain Ravi was no longer in the corridor, Blue returned to Toria's office. They hadn't even stopped in to visit Petite; they'd hardly been in any kind of headspace to talk with anyone.

Thankfully, Toria was alone in her office when Blue arrived.

"What's wrong?" Toria asked, swiping the desk screen off and focusing her attention on Blue.

"Maybe I just came to give the mission briefing."

Toria gestured at the seat opposite her but Blue lingered where they stood. "You're welcome to go ahead with your deception and give me a full mission briefing, if that's what you want."

"I was right outside the library and I got recognised."

It had been terrifying, Blue's emotional surge blocked clicked in their chest at even the memory of it.

Major Alitin had aged since the last time Blue had seen him, as humans tended to do. His hair had gone from its light brown to grey. Lines decorated his forehead and the areas around his eyes. His ubiquitous uniform was nowhere to be found, not that that meant much about his current status with the military and H4H. There was no lingering evidence of where Blue had punched him – but what kind of evidence could they have left from a flailing punch in a desperate attempt to flee?

He had waggled his finger at Blue and said, "I know you. You're that cyborg from Station 132."

"No," Blue had argued. "You're mistaken."

"Yes you are. I remember the way you used to dance for me." His eyes had roamed over them like a physical touch.

"Are you honestly telling me you think I'm a cyborg?" Blue had tried to laugh.

Major Alitin's hand had flashed out to grab Blue's wrist.

They whipped it away. "Leave me alone, old man."

He stepped in close, breath washing over Blue in a wave of unpleasant temperature and humidity. Standing just as closed as he had used to. Just as close as all the times he had crowded Blue up into a wall, his hand wrapping tightly around their throat. "You think I wouldn't recognise a filthy Pleasure Bot?"

Blue had bolted.

"And then," they told Toria. "I ended up running down a side street and climbing an open bin to hide on a roof until the night cycle."

"So he just wanted to trade you in?"

"Something like that," Blue hedged. Why was it that they could never quite find the words to tell Toria what they had been designed for? Technically they'd never *told* anyone. Everyone who knew had figured it out for themself. For all Blue knew, Toria had already figured it out and was just trying to be polite by not bringing it up.

But Blue was scared. Ravi's reaction hadn't exactly been reassuring. Blue exhaled. They shifted around to Toria's side of the desk and hooped to sit on it. "Ravi knows me from before."

Toria jerked. "How?"

"It's complicated. He knew me before The Crash."

"Shit. Blue, are you okay?"

A rich question. One they couldn't answer. How could they possibly be okay? Having to fight for their very existence every day. Having to be reminded of their inhumanity every time their battery ran low. Having people know their past, the past they weren't ashamed of but would still rather keep to themself. People would look at them differently if they knew, people always did. Even Isa didn't know. Even Isa would see them in a different, more colour-wiped lighting if she found out.

"See, this is why I keep saying to stop bringing people here."

"It is not," Blue argued easily.

"You're right. But still, loose lips sink ships."

With thoughtless habit, Blue reached for the communal databank, gutted to find it empty still. "I don't know that one."

"It's an ancient idiom from the home world. It means the more people who know a secret, the less of a secret it is and the more danger it brings. It *means* what happens if this H4H pilot isn't as trustworthy as you seem to think he is? Or have you changed your mind now that you know what he used to be like?"

"He died, Toria! Do you really think he's holding himself to the people who got him killed?"

Toria threw her hands up. "Why can I never get you to see things from my perspective?"

Blue surged to their feet and laid their hands on her

desk. "That's pretty fucking rich, Toria, considering that you won't see things from mine either."

"Then tell me yours."

For an instant, Blue stalled. How did one even go about verbalising perspective? Blue had always been able to share, to upload to the Mainframe before, when they wanted to share such a personal experience. The concept of putting it into words was so unfathomable that Blue almost couldn't remember how to form words at all. "If we don't protect everyone, how are we better than the people we're resisting?"

"If we bring in everyone who claims they need help without vetting them at all, how can we keep the people we promised to protect safe?" Toria countered.

Blue blew out a breath, wishing once again that they could sigh like a human. She had a point. "I'll keep an eye on him. He spends all his time with Petite anyway."

"That... works." Toria leaned her elbow on the desk, resting her chin in her hand. "How did we not come up with that earlier?"

Blue laughed. "I don't know. I think we were both too wrapped up in our own thoughts on the matter to be able to communicate."

Toria sighed. "This is so much harder than I thought it would be."

"It's all I've ever known."

"I forget that you didn't get to choose to be here."

"Technically neither did you."

Toria smiled. "It is different for me. As much as I want to stand up for people like me, people with mechanical prosthetics, I could have stood by, nobody was coming for me yet. You, on the other hand, you're the forewarning."

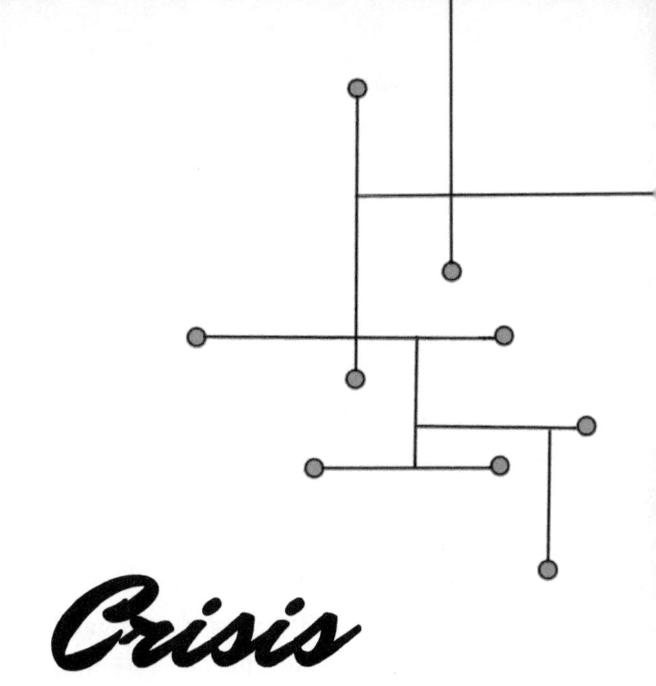

Crisis

Welcome To The Mission
Ravi

Piloting the ship proved easier than Ravi thought it would. His theoretical knowledge of having been a pilot wasn't guaranteed to match up with his current capabilities, and yet, as soon as he sat in the pilot's chair, instinct had kicked in.

Once they were docked in one of the ports, he spun the pilot's chair around to inform the other members of his team.

Blue didn't glance up from the floor plans of the Residential Station even as Petite emerged from the back room. "Don't ask me if I'm charged," Blue warned her.

Petite snorted but her nerves were palpable.

"You look different," Blue accused.

She had swapped her usual tank top and cargo pants for a jumper and skirt combo. She pulled the long sleeves over her hands. Even her hair was out of its usual loose waves, instead tied in a pair of bunches just behind her ears. She looked young in a way that made Ravi distinctly uncomfortable. "I am technically a fugitive."

"I know. I could kill them for putting this on you."

Petite sighed, glancing sideways at the map Blue had

been poring over. "It makes sense, with the new scanners in place at the quadri libraries; they needed someone without any mech."

"Bet you're regretting your snooty attitude to it now," Blue teased.

"I can't help it if I only want the best possible choices – what would have been the point of an enhancement that needed to recharge after heart-beat chargers appeared?"

Blue laughed even as their shoulders tightened with the same tension running through Ravi. "Yes, you look lovely all the way up on that tall tree. You want to go over the plan?"

"We need to be quick," Ravi interjected. "We're already docked."

"Fuck, Ravi, I didn't even notice. You're a good pilot."

Pride swelled in Ravi's chest. It was good to hear he was skilled at something since his Re-Animation.

"It'll be fine, Blue," Petite reassured. "I've lived on a quadri, they're all laid out the same."

Blue nodded vaguely.

Petite pulled Blue into her arms, wrapping them in a fierce hug. Blue's fingers dug into the fabric of the jumper at the small of her back.

And then she dipped out the shuttle door.

"Don't worry," Ravi said. "Everything will be fine."

Blue glanced at him, tapped their fingers against each other, shot him a guilty look and surged out of the 'ship door into the docking bay.

Ravi was halfway across the ship before he realised there was no benefit to his joining in on the mission dissent. What would his visible presence off-ship, on station do to aid the situation? Nothing. He would be an extra risk and it wasn't worth adding extra risks to an already risky mission.

As much as Blue had fought his corner in his meeting with Toria, he hadn't expected to be invited onto a mission so soon, especially with Blue avoiding him since the revelation about them being a cyb'.

Ravi had been hesitant to approach Isa for help reconciling it, but he couldn't face the thought of asking Petite, who so obviously loved Blue with her whole heart even if she wasn't willing to admit it outright. So he had steeled himself and asked Isa for help.

She'd laughed at him for taking so long to figure it out since Blue was apparently not at all interested in hiding it. But after that she'd offered him real comfort and advice. She'd told him she didn't want to own her past life, that it wasn't who she was now and that she didn't know if it was the same for Blue.

"What you're feeling," she'd said. "That awkward uncertainty because you knew them before they were Blue, they're feeling the same but with the added fear that you, their new friend, might see them differently or might even not want to be their friend anymore because of a life they had no control over."

"I wouldn't!" Ravi had protested.

Isa had shrugged. "It's not about you but proving that to Blue might be a good idea."

"How? They're avoiding me."

"Give them time."

When Toria had given him this mission, Ravi had hoped he would be able to talk with Blue. Especially since they were just there as backup for Petite.

Ravi's mechanical hand formed and released a fist. He

watched the fingers move, so lifelike and yet so alien.

Ravi couldn't have begun to say how long it was before Petite crashed back onto the 'ship.

"Where's Blue?"

"Drawing off the soldiers." Petite couldn't pry her eyes away from the shuttle door.

"Soldiers?"

"I got recognised. I bumped into someone from my old life, a researcher on one of the projects I used to work on. He recognised me, called me out in the middle of the square. Called for KTPOs." She looked at Ravi with wide, panicked eyes. "So I ran. And I got cornered, dipped down the wrong alley, couldn't get out. And then Blue appeared. They just hopped down in front of me and told me where to go and that they were going to draw the attention of the soldiers. That they were a bigger prize than me."

"When they realise you've got away they'll ground all 'ships," Ravi warned.

"We're not leaving Blue!"

"You think I was suggesting that! I meant can you hack into the radio?"

"Don't you know the frequency?"

"I don't remember. It's not that simple."

"Right." She wiped her hands over her face then tugged the ties out of her bunches and pulled her hair up into a bun. "It's more like muscle memory, right?"

"Right..."

"So, when you get on a 'ship you go to your station and...?"

Ravi huffed out a breath but settled into his chair. "Run a systems check." He closed his eyes, hands flicking out to press the appropriate buttons. He groaned. "Say something mean about cyborgs."

"They're... not human?" Petite offered, confused.

"They're lying in wait to take over, Simtiv." Ravi snarked in an imitation of his old General. "Haven't you seen the Terminator movies, Simtiv?" His fingers flashed over buttons, starting up processes and, finally, flicking on the radio, turning the dial until static changed to voices. "Await orders," Ravi finished in his own voice.

His shoulders slumped and he rubbed his face, exhausted. A clear voice rang through the speakers.

"Apprehended one third generation 'borg. Repeat, apprehended one third generation 'borg. Fugitive still on the loose."

"They have Blue," Petite whispered.

Welcome To Rebuild
Pink

"You can't just keep bringing people here left, right, and centre!" the pink haired woman who had not bothered to introduce herself snapped at the cyborg.

"She's a mechanic," the cyborg argued back. "You said you wanted a mechanic!"

"She hardly looks like a mechanic." She sighed. "You're going to be the death of me one of these days, Blue."

"At least you'll die with my stunning face in your mind. A little comfort."

The pink haired woman snorted a laugh and turned her attention back to the screened desk below her. "Take her to Isa, I guess. Let Isa figure out what to do with another mouth to feed."

Blue turned away from the pink haired woman and stared out of the office. "Come on you," they invited. "Let's get you to Isa and we can do the grand tour later."

Pink followed.

As soon as the door slid shut, Blue said, "Don't mind Toria, she thinks she's in charge but we're a democracy here."

Pink nodded vaguely.

Blue led her down a series of corridors, the plexi-sheets that made up the walls were yellowed with age, almost so yellow that Pink wondered that they had ever been white at all. But that was foolish, all walls were white. Atop the yellowing plexi and uncomfortably red-stained floor, there was paint. It started outside Toria's office with a few delicately painted flowers, and one sunflower with a smiling face in the broad strokes of either a child or at least someone unused to holding a paint brush.

As they shifted into the more used portions of the station, more and more paint adorned the walls. Pictures at various heights drawn straight onto it in ink or paint. Hand prints of various sizes and in various hues. One caught Pink's eye, appearing to be the central heart from which all the other hand prints and drawings extended. One that almost graced the ceiling with how high on the wall it was placed, slightly faded, printed red soil.

She glanced at Blue, examining the size and shape of their hands, wondering if it was them who had first adorned these walls.

Isa, as it turned out, was another cyborg. A Gen-2 bordering on Gen-3. All the appearance of a Gen-3 typical service bot but the lack of mouth movement more typical of Gen-2. The sides of her head were green panels, disconcerting next to her humanoid face. Her hands were entirely green, though the rest of her was covered by her clothing, a delicate floral shirt and loose leg trousers that made Pink think of skirts.

"You look half-starved," she greeted, grabbing a plexi plate and loading it up with food for Pink.

Before Pink could dig in, Isa put a hand on her shoulder. "Take it slow if it's been a while."

As Pink dug into the food, all perfectly made, well-seasoned and fresh in a way she really wasn't accustomed to, the two cyborgs chatted.

"How pissed it Toria?" Isa asked, leaning against the table in a casual manner.

"Is that a real question?" Blue responded, hopping up to sit on the table Pink wasn't eating at.

"You'd think she'd have a little more respect for your choices seeing as she was one."

"She's just scared."

"I don't care. Come on, Blue, you're the one constantly risking your own safety as if you weren't already the most at risk."

"It's not that bad."

"Oh, sure!" Somehow, even without mouth movement, and with the mechanical hum that accompanied Isa's voice, the words came out sarcastic. "Because you're only worth a brand new Gen-5 cyb or cash equivalent if someone trades you in."

"Wait what?" Pink blurted.

"Didn't you know?" Isa asked. "Gen-3 cybes can be traded in for a literal reward."

"Why?"

Blue rolled their eyes. "Because of The Crash and all the bullshit surrounding it. Can we not talk about this? You ragging on me isn't going to stop Toria asking me to go out and it's not going to make me refuse her either. Instead, let's celebrate the fact that I brought you..." they dug into their belt pouch. "A maguffin!"

"A heat coil replacement."

"Probably." They tossed the thing at Isa who caught it easily. "But better yet." They gestured at Pink like she was a miraculous thing even as she tried to slorp up the long piece of vegetable – real vegetable not vegetable broth powder! – hanging half out of her mouth. "I brought you a mechanic!"

Isa bodily turned to Pink. "Really?"

Pink swallowed. "Yeah, my specialism is life-mechanics and the integration of mechanical and biological systems but... Yes. Mechanic. That's me."

"Oh I could kiss you!" Isa gushed. "Both of you!"

As soon as Pink finished her plate, Isa herded her toward the cooker to install the heat coil replacement.

It turned out to be an easy enough task, even if it did include sliding under the cooker – cool and unplugged – like an upside down lizard. She twisted the spanner in the relative dark, working more by feel than sight as the new heat coil slipped into the recently vacated spot of the old one with the ease of a part designed for purpose.

Here was hoping it hadn't been in the junkyard because it was broken.

Pink wriggled back out from underneath.

Something clattered from her tool belt to the floor.

"Oh, your screw driver," Isa said. "Oops, it's broken."

Pink sat up so fast she thwacked her head against the edge of the cooker. "I need that!"

"Okay," Isa laughed. "Sorry." She handed over the screw driver, the end that Pink had pried off that first day on the run nowhere to be found and the chip from inside missing too.

"Shit!" Pink hissed, shoving the tool in her belt and scrambling around on her hands and knees looking for the chip.

"What's wrong?" Isa asked.

"I can't– I don't–"

She couldn't risk that chip falling into the wrong hands. Even just good-natured Resistance hands would be too risky. What if they plugged it into something to see what it was? They'd find the data *and* her previous identity and, as if that wouldn't be bad enough in itself, the information, all that carefully stolen and destroyed data about memory reset chips for Re-Ans, would be uploaded to the Mainframe for anyone to access.

Anyone, including Nikolai.

Welcome To Reset
Blue

The voice faded in and out of comprehension as Blue adjusted to the latest reboot. Blue had always been slow after a restart, something about being Gen-3 Alpha and a non-typical service bot. It was always worse after allowing their power cells to drain too far.

"Petite?" Blue murmured around lips they couldn't quite feel.

Silence followed the question. Blue's memory booted. No. Petite wouldn't be here.

Blue had been beyond restless as soon as the door had closed behind Petite. They had tried and failed to start several conversations with Ravi before they'd dipped out the door and climbed the radio tower to keep an eye on Petite.

It wasn't that Blue didn't trust Petite. But Ravi was an ex-military pilot, he had combat training that he could fall back on in a way Petite just... didn't.

They had followed Petite across the quadri's streets, from one rooftop to another, dipping down into secluded corners and utilising ledges and windows to stay out of view.

It hadn't taken too long for Petite to disappear into the library, or to emerge back out through those huge sweeping doors. She started down the ramp into the main square when a human in a suit hesitated as Petite passed him. He and Petite exchanged a few words, too far away for Blue to hear and at the wrong angle to read lips.

Petite had backed away. The other human grabbed at her.

Blue's limbs had tensed, ready to leap to her aid. But Blue wasn't foolish, they knew better than to go leaping to their own demise for Petite's defence. The scanner mounted to the library doors would scan them, register a Gen-3 cyb', and set off the alarms. Besides, maybe Petite could handle it alone. Toria and the Resistance council obviously thought she could.

Alarms blared anyway, and Blue cursed themself for not immediately leaping to Petite's aid. They scrambled to follow Petite's haphazard dash through the streets before dropping down in front of her.

Ravi would have got Petite out of there, right?

As each of Blue's units came back online, piece by piece, limb by limb, they realised something was very wrong. Blue squinted down at the wires connecting them to the Mainframe. It was a Gen Delta-H2 Mainframe Connection Unit. The closest thing to Blue's era that still functioned with any reliability. Gen-3 Mainframe Connection Units had become corrupted by The Crash or destroyed after it.

A scientist stood beside it. He muttered to himself, or possibly into a Dictaphone. Either way, Blue was fairly certain he wasn't talking to them. "Subject seems to be resisting reset. Looks to be an M47713."

Blue couldn't help the snort that escaped them. This

guy was clearly old enough to have lived through The Crash and yet he couldn't tell an M4 from an 87?

He stared down at Blue as if he couldn't believe that they were awake, or that they were laughing at him.

"Report," he demanded.

"You'll have to be more specific." Blue tried for a casual tone and smile.

"State your designation and purpose."

"My designation is screw you and my purpose is none of your business."

"Subject shows no sign of standardised behaviour. Attempting once more."

Pain washed through Blue as the reset was attempted. They kept their mouth shut to avoid crying out. Cyborgs weren't designed to feel pain.

Resets hadn't used to hurt. It had been a part of the charging matrix. Every few days, Blue had connected to the Mainframe. Their learnt information was uploaded to the communal databank and any individuality was wiped out, reset to match everyone else. Until The Crash. Now everything Blue had learnt was theirs and theirs alone.

The Crash really had changed everything.

"State your designation."

"My designation is go suck on a di–"

Pain, blackness, fuzzy awakening.

"State your designation."

"Go die in a hole!"

Pain, blackness, fuzzy awakening.

"State your designation."

"Fuck you."

Pain, this time Blue couldn't quite keep it to themself. Blackness. Fuzzy awakening.

"State your designation."

Blue gritted their teeth against the pain coursing through them. The buzzing in their ears was hard to focus past. They imagined it was similar to when humans could hear their own heartbeats. "My designation?" They asked. "What's your designation?"

Pain. Something cried out as Blue fell into blackness once again.

"State your designation."

Blue's vision was tinged with colours. Someone had been playing with their graphics chip. This idiot probably thought it was a memory board. Gen-3 Alpha had weird design compared to most other cybes. It was an easy mistake to make if you weren't used to it. Either that, or the repeated resets with the wrong Mainframe Connection Unit were flushing too much power through Blue's systems and corrupting their wires.

"87113." Blue's voice was soft. Self-preservation was an odd thing. Sometimes Blue wondered if it was as useful as humans seemed to think it was. Could they even call it a human trait since it had basically been running Blue's life since they left the Pleasure House?

"State your purpose," the scientist demanded.

Blue didn't need to look at him to feel the satisfaction pouring off him. The closed their eyes. If Blue had been a human they might have cried. But cybes weren't installed with tear ducts.

"I was programmed to serve whatever purpose the designated human gives me."

Whoever had set that up was either a manipulative idiot who didn't care, way too naive, or wanted to be able to demand exactly what they wanted of a cyb' with no consequences.

The scientist started muttering again. Blue turned to look at him, vision still flooded with rainbows and soft patches of pastels. When had the second scientist appeared? This one tall with dark brown hair, peering down at Blue with full lips pulled into a sneer.

The pair chatted too softly for Blue to make out.

"Tell me about the fugitive," the second scientist demanded.

He meant Petite. "I cannot." The bitter taste in Blue's mouth didn't surprise them, being able to keep it out of their voice did.

"You've fried its memory circuits!" the second scientist snapped at the first.

Blue turned away from the bickering humans. Their memory circuits were just fine. "They," they murmured. "Not it."

The scientists left, turning off the lights in the lab. Blue counted to one hundred before deciding to try moving. There was no point beginning an escape only to be caught just outside the door.

As they pushed themself into a sitting position they wanted to scream. How corrupted had their wires become? How much damage had been done to them in this facility? How many times had they been reset? How long had they been here?

The pulled the connection wires from their limbs, closing over sections that should never have been opened and clenching their jaw to try and keep themself quiet and calm. They slid the door open a crack, peeking out into an empty corridor.

Limping out into the hallway, Blue tried to ignore the

way their limbs functioned on a delay, tried to ignore the blaring of their internal sensors. Their left leg was malfunctioning. Their right leg was malfunctioning. Everything was broken or damaged, and every malfunction wanted to be known and categorised.

The lights buzzed, a warning that they had sensed movement and were heartbeats from blinking to life. Blue scrambled to press their fingers against the energy blocker in their boot, clenching their jaw against the electric jolt of pain that blasted its way through them.

The bare corridor opened up into a huge space with eight rows of desks evenly laid out with five desks a row. Each one sat tidy and neat, glittering with the sheen of port-screen surfaces. Toria would love resources like this. Why was a cyb' reset facility so decked out? Surely they didn't need forty people working at desks, not even beginning to count the rooms Blue had walked past.

Blue almost wished they hadn't used the disruptor at all, that they could have investigated what someone was doing at one of those desks. Curiosity swarming through them, Blue pressed on into the room. It took too long for them to notice the sound of a pen squeaking on glass. When Blue finally realised the sound wasn't just their damaged electrical circuitry, they turned toward it.

A man stood inside a plexi-glass cubicle, one of the scientists that had been in the lab with Blue, the one who had accused the other of frying Blue's circuits. His arm moved with the pen squeaks, writing on the clear walls of the cubicle.

Blue froze. Their limbs locked.

What was he doing here so late in the day-night cycle?

The scientist had a light shining from his porti-screen

onto the plexi-glass but as he shifted to another side of the walls and the main light didn't respond, he hesitated, pen-hand falling to sit just below his shoulder. He turned toward the centre of the room.

Blue dropped to the floor. Rather, Blue tried. Their damaged circuits didn't react.

Blue stood, frozen to the spot as the scientist locked his eyes on them.

Rescue

Welcome To Infiltration
Ravi

The night cycle lights were engaged throughout the station, illuminating areas dimly whenever the sensors registered movement. Ravi led Petite through the dim space. A bland corridor, round a corner to another bland corridor. Their footsteps were loud in the silence of the station.

Ravi hesitated, peeking around a corner before rounding it. It opened up into a huge square room filled with desks. A plexi-glass cubicle sat in one corner. Halfway across the room, Ravi registered the lack of secondary footsteps.

Petite stood frozen in the centre of the room, staring at the cubicle.

That tiny office wasn't an inbuilt feature; its ceiling sat a fair way below the actual roof. What was it that bothered her so much? Ravi couldn't find the voice to ask beyond the sensation of his heart racing in his throat – despite the very even beats of his mechanical heart.

The last time he had been on a mission like this he had literally died.

Petite crept over to examine the equations scrawled across the glass. She pulled the door to the cubicle open.

Ravi dashed between desks. "What are you doing?" he hissed.

Petite grabbed an empty, reusable plexi-sheet from the top of the desk and started copying down equations. "These formulae..." Petite muttered in answer to Ravi. "They're... a new concept. I just want to see where it leads."

"We're here for a reason," Ravi pressed even as Petite flicked through the plexi-sheets on the desk.

She pressed a key code into the plate on one drawer. It beeped and slid open. How did she know the code?

These days, it was rare to print anything – an unsustainable practice. But some high level, important documents were printed for paranoia about the information being lost somewhere in the expanse of the Mainframe. The drawer held a folder of just such printouts. They all read the same across the top, "Dr Palmer's Recovered Research."

"We need to find Blue and get out of here. Now." Petite grabbed all the printouts and her plexi-sheet of notes, swiped an elbow across some of the writing on the wall and dashed from the cubicle.

The lights in the next corridor didn't flash to life. Ravi hesitated in the entryway. The sensors didn't glow with a sustained red pinprick. In fact, it didn't seem to have any power at all. Someone had used an energy blocker in this corridor. And recently.

The only light visible streamed out from the edges of a door.

Something pinned Ravi to the floor even as Petite continued to hurry forward. She slid the door open.

His back to them, a tall scientist with deep brown hair cut short worked on a project cyb'. He'd peeled its synthetic skin back, blue oil – life fluid – leaked from it. Must be a hyper realistic cyb to be leaking machine oil, unless they all did that? After all, they'd stopped making hyper-realistic cybes after The Crash.

The scientist shifted to one side and Ravi couldn't help the small choked gasp that escaped him as the cyb's foot twitched in an all too human motion. Pain. They were in pain.

Wire stretched from various machines – a Gen-2 Mainframe Connection Unit, a reset box, a code unscrambler, and more beyond what Ravi could name – toward the body on the table. They poked into the cyb's limbs, their exposed, open limbs.

"Nikolai," Petite breathed.

Nikolai turned to face Ravi and Petite where they stood in the dimness of the hallway. A dark look crossed his face as he stepped aside, sweeping an arm over the body. "Care to take a shot, Doctor? This circuitry is unparalleled. It almost reminds me of someone I used to work with – how long has it been?"

Doctor?

"Please. I would love your notes on my work. You never had any qualms sharing before." He stepped away from the table. "Show me you still have what made me recruit you."

Recruit her? Recruit her for what? When? Petite was a double agent?

Welcome To Your Old Life
Petite

Petite, almost as if compelled, stepped into the lab. Maybe it was fear. Maybe it was habit. Maybe it was the fact that she had never seen such intricately worked circuity, not all opened up like this. This cyb' must have been made before The Crash, well before. Before any promises about Gen-4 or the never-built but oft-promised Gen-5. So much of the information to build these intricate circuits and machines had been lost to time and fear and paranoia.

Petite had always wanted to focus on bio-engineering, working with mechanics for humans, rather than the cybernetic and cyborg side of things. But even she had to admit, there was a beauty in this that no organic creature quite matched. Bio-mechanics were messy by necessity; they had to fit to what was already there. This was art.

Her eyes roamed hungrily over the hyper-lifelike flesh, the mimicry of veins and arteries up the arms and legs. She was both glad and disappointed to find that the torso had not been disturbed yet.

The cyb's chest rose and fell, breathing in and out. What was the purpose of such a feature? Did it change dependant on exertion levels? Could this cyb' suffocate? Isa had to remember to mimic breathing, but that obviously wasn't an issue for this cyb'. Petite could count the number of cybes with such a feature on one hand.

As she circled the cyb' on the table, Petite noted the right arm differed from the left. She paused to examine it more closely.

Someone had damaged this circuitry, and repaired it but in a worse state than it had been before. Maybe she could fix it properly. Maybe she could at least try. Her hands itched to grab at her tool belt, but she'd left it on the Resistance Base for the mission that had gone so horribly wrong.

Life oil dripped slowly onto the floor at the head of the table. The furthest end from the door. The cyb's head hung off the head of the table, throat opened up, blue blood coating the entire face, leaking into their choppy hair, hanging down off their face due to the angle.

Petite's heart stopped.

"Problem, Dr Palmer?"

Petite stumbled away from the table, hand flashing up to cover her mouth lest she vomit.

How could she have let curiosity get the better of her? How long had it taken to slip back into the person she had been the last time she'd seen Nikolai? Seconds? Maybe a minute at most and she was examining a cyborg like an object rather than a person. Would she even have realised she was doing it if she hadn't noticed it was this particular cyb'?

Nikolai's hands clamped around her upper arms. "A shame," he breathed over her shoulder. "I really did see your promise once upon a time."

An alarm blared.

Petite tried to fight her way out of his hold as armed security grabbed hold of Ravi.

"While you're here," Nikolai said, conversationally, to one of the officers. "Take this useless machine to recycling."

"No!" Petite screamed, but it was too late.

Welcome To The Precipice
Blue

The first time Petite had kissed Blue was a few weeks after she had joined the Resistance. Blue had been out on a mission and returned with, not only what they were sent for, but a ream of mildly used copper wiring. After debriefing with Toria, they'd headed to the engineering lab Petite had claimed and offered it up.

Petite had extracted herself from a pieced together generator with a beaming grin. She'd grabbed Blue's face between her hands and pressed his lips briefly against Blue's own. "How did you know?" She'd asked, taking the wire and disappearing back inside the generator.

It had been nothing like any of the many kisses Blue had experienced in the past. Those had always had connotations of expected future activities, or current ones. Never a brief, chaste kiss like Blue had seen humans give one another.

Still, it set Blue on edge. They were a non-typical service bot, and they looked the part. There was the risk that she'd only done it because of that.

But what if she hadn't?

The second time Petite kissed Blue was softer. She found them charging in the old 'ship that had probably started this whole planet.

Her arrival had startled Blue out of the dazed, power-saving state they slipped into while charging – never fully at rest these days, not since the virus. Blue pressed a hand over where they were plugged into the ship, hiding the cable, hiding their single exposed band.

She'd hesitated in the doorway. "Is this... Is this the parts mobile?"

"No."

"Fuck. Sorry, I'll leave you in peace."

"Wait!"

Petite turned.

Blue let their head flop down, hiding from her inquisitive gaze. Why had they called her back? "What part were you looking for?"

"We can discuss this later?" Petite suggested. "When you're not... busy."

"Busy?"

"I didn't want to say charging since you're so obviously hiding the wire."

Blue chuckled. "Badly, it seems."

Petite shrugged. "I'm just observant for this kind of thing. Did you... did you want me to stay?"

Blue wanted to refuse; the sensible thing would be to ask her to leave, to stay in this awful bubble of loneliness with no communal databank, no community, no connection.

Petite slid down the opposite wall, sitting across from Blue and crossing her legs underneath her. "When I was a kid, my friends and I would sit like this in my bedroom – it was tiny, I grew up on a hexi, they're the most densely populated of the Stations so the houses tend to be smaller. But me and my friends all lived the same way and I didn't have any siblings so they came over to my house and we used to sit like this and tell stories about what we wanted our futures to look like."

Blue smiled. "Tell me your story, then."

"I wanted to be an engineer –"

"No," Blue interrupted. "Tell me your story for the future."

That had stumped Petite.

"Mine is connection," Blue said. "And autonomy."

"It's supposed to be more like 'I'll get married and have twenty babies' or something."

Blue threw their head back in a laugh.

"No," Petite protested, cheeks flaming. "I mean like a proper picture, not general statements."

"Sorry," Blue offered around lingering snickers. "Okay. I want to walk down the street without having to look over my shoulder. I want to live a life like those I've seen other people do. A house and a garden and neighbours I know the names of."

Petite leaned her head back against the wall. "Yeah..." she sighed. "That sounds nice. That and someone to share that with."

They spent the next few hours chatting and swapping stories and making each other laugh until Blue's internal battery sensor chimed to alert Blue that they were fully charged. Blue stared down at the wire connecting them into the 'ship.

Fully charged? They hadn't been fully charged since... Since before The Crash.

"You okay?" Petite asked.

"Yeah," Blue answered, still distractedly staring down at their arm.

Petite levered to her feet. "I should get back to it." She pressed soft lips against Blue's forehead and jogged back across the red soil.

Blue's fingers traced where Petite's lips had been. Forehead. What was the purpose of a forehead kiss? What was the meaning behind it?

The third time Petite had kissed Blue was in Blue's suite. She had turned up at Blue's door, at Blue's request. They had needed to speak with her alone, had found a datachip with incriminating information on it, including a personnel profile listing Petite as a doctoral engineer with a surname.

Blue hadn't told anyone about the information yet, had barely looked at it themself. Had wanted to give Petite the opportunity to explain for herself.

She'd let her hair down from its usual bun, the soft waves falling past her shoulders. "What's up?"

"I..." Blue had trailed off.

Petite's shoulders and arms were exposed by the grey and black tank top she wore, muscles highlighted by the dim light in Blue's suite – Blue hardly needed much by way of lighting. Her hands sat in the pockets of her cargo pants. She hadn't brought her tool belt. Blue couldn't remember the last time they'd seen her without her tool belt.

"I wanted to see how you're doing," they said. "How you're settling into the Resistance."

Petite settled herself on the aged sofa in the centre of the suite. "Toria sure is an acquired taste."

Blue settled next to her, pulling one leg up onto the seat to turn their whole body toward her.

"But other than that it's been great."

Blue was good at reading humans. They'd been

designed for it: designed to learn, and inbuilt with typical expectations. Earnest was one of those things humans struggled to fake and there was so much of it around Petite's delivery of those words.

"You're happy here?" Blue asked.

Petite's mouth curved into a soft smile. "Definitely."

That was answer enough. Blue shoved the chip into the couch cushions. "I'm glad."

Petite glanced at them. "Was that... all?"

Blue trailed their fingertips down Petite's cheek, under the scar that slashed across her cheekbone. "I did also want to ask," they voice came out soft, almost a whisper. "About the kisses."

Petite wet her lips. "Kisses?"

"Are you just... like that with everyone? Affectionate? Casual intimacy?"

Petite shook her head almost imperceptibly but for Blue's fingers still on her cheek.

"Then why?"

She looked up at Blue from under her lashes.

This time it was Blue that kissed her. This kiss was, just like all the others shared with Petite thus far, completely unique to Blue. Completely alien. It felt like they were perched on the very edge of something, wind whistling and catching in their hair and clothes. As if they were at the very edge of a station, staring out into the limitless void, only the gravitational pull, only the falsified atmosphere keeping them rooted. As if, if they took one step forward they would fly out, or fall to their doom.

Petite's hand landed on their arm, their blue bands, uncovered for a change. An anchor, something to cling to. Someone to spend their hoped for life with.

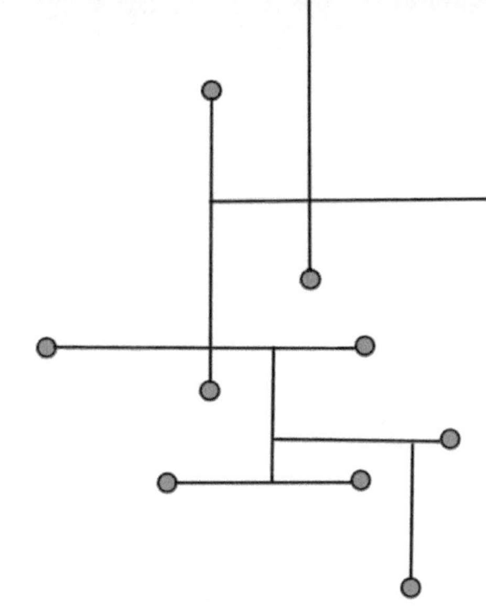

Questioning

Welcome To Your New Life
Ravi

Ravi gasped. Pain flared through him. His vision blurred in the sudden bright light. Hands held him down.

Combat training kicked in.

By the time his vision had cleared he was holding a doctor pinned to a small table of instruments.

Ah, a screwdriver.

Wait. Why was he back in the Re-An centre?

At least his limbs mostly worked this time. Even if Petite couldn't fix them perfectly, even if they still ached and malfunctioned and would for the rest of his life, at least they stood and moved mostly as he wanted them to.

Oh, shit, Petite.

He let go of the doctor and stepped back. Boxy white walls surrounded him, no windows to be found. The strip lights bolted over the ceiling gave his vision stripes of odd colours, or maybe that was just a by-product of medical unconsciousness, however that had happened. Last thing he remembered was finding out Petite was once called Dr Palmer and had once been recruited by the scientist experimenting on Blue.

His eyebrows furrowed as he tried to remember.

"Some confusion is normal," the doctor said in a bored tone. Was this just how they ran things? "Can you tell me your name?"

"Ravi."

"You're taking this very well, Ravi."

That was probably a fair assessment, especially considering how he'd taken it last time. But, then again, he hadn't actually been Re-Animated this time.

"Welcome to your new life, Ravi. You have been Re-Animated at the request of the military. As you know, I cannot divulge any information about your past. Your memories have been sealed away by an implant chip in your brain and any attempt to discover information about your old life could cause issues with the Re-An process." Xe swiped on xyr porti-screen. "Since you remember your first name, you are welcome to continue using it, or another can be assigned to you."

"Wait," Ravi interrupted.

"Sorry, can't." Again, the doctor didn't sound very sorry at all. "You're designated twenty minutes and I haven't even started the physical yet."

When Ravi ended up in what might as well have been the exact same N-RAS waiting room as the one in which he'd met Blue, whether it had been repaired or this was a different one hardly mattered, he dug his fingernails into the skin of his right, synthetic wrist. He peeled it back just enough to reveal the burned out, blood stained memory chip Petite had removed from his head on their first meeting.

Good.

He pressed the skin back down, hiding the chip back in the empty spot it stayed in. That meant the memories with the Resistance hadn't been some kind of half-dead hallucination. All his memories of the Resistance, Blue, and Petite seemed to be intact too, so it was unlikely he had been provided a new memory chip. Which also meant the people here thought his chip was still intact.

What in the name of the Central Mainframe was going on here?

Once again his eye was drawn to the 'Welcome To Your New Life' poster.

Before too long a man in military uniform appeared through the door. He carried himself in a way that demonstrated his combat training and power. His light brown hair, streaked with grey, had been tied back in a ponytail slightly longer than military regulations would normally allow.

"Hello," Major Alitin greeted in a disgusting attempt at a soft voice. Ravi had seen him on duty, shared a squad with him, seen his preferences in Pleasure Houses. There was nothing soft about this man. "I'm Major Alitin, you probably don't remember me."

Ravi kept his mouth shut.

"You're a war hero, Sim–" he cleared his throat. "Ravi."

"War hero?"

"Yes, in our war against the cyborg uprising."

"What am I supposed to do about it?"

"We think you can sneak into their base."

Oh, so they intended to use his Re-An life to their advantage, assuming Ravi had no memory of it. How was he going to get out of that? As much as he wanted to return to the Resistance, to see if Blue or Petite had managed to escape the horrors that had him trapped in the Re-An centre, to see if Toria would mount another mission to get them both back, he couldn't risk leading the military right to the base. But if they thought he had no memory, how was he supposed to take them back to the base anyway?

Ravi might be confused but he wasn't stupid, he knew better than to think the military would let him go so easily this time around.

If they had even let him go the last time. If his Re-An life thus far hadn't been a plan concocted by the military in the first place.

What if someone like Major Alitin had set Blue and Petite up with the leaked information in the Re-An centre specifically so they could run into Ravi, so they might pick him up and take him with them, so Ravi *could* eventually be used as a double agent? What if they were working on the idea that he was going to wake up with just as much loyalty to the military as he had died with, that he would eventually come back because they couldn't understand a way in which Ravi would ever see cybes as people, as *human?*

Welcome To Interrogation Room V
Petite

The room was nicer than Petite had expected. A pair of soft sofas with fabric – not plexi-leather, but honest to orbit fabric – coated plush cushions took up most of the space. A squat table perched between them with a pair of water glasses atop it. Petite didn't need to pick up either glass to know they would be shatter proof. There was no way Nikolai would take that kind of risk. Not with her. Not now.

The whole situation so reminiscent of their first meeting. Luxury surroundings to create the exact balance of intimidation Nikolai wanted, if only Petite had been wise or experienced enough to see it the first time, instead of enamoured with the whole idea. Instead of flattered that someone so capable wanted to lavish her with his attention. Instead of caught up in the idea that she would take yet another step up in the hierarchy. Now, instead of being something she could aspire toward, the luxury was a reminder of what she had traded away. It was intended to instil fear and regret. Even the pristine whiteness of the walls told Petite how well maintained this space was. No wear and tear showed on any surface.

And it was bland and boring and without any semblance of personality. It made her long for the painted walls of the Resistance base.

Petite sank down on the nearest sofa, the weight of her guilt pressing against her. Blue... And it was all Petite's fault. It was always her fault. The guilt mixed nauseatingly with the anxiety turning her legs to jelly.

How could she have let this happen? How could Blue be gone?

Recycled.

She dropped her head into her hands. Could she have done anything more to keep them safe?

And what about Ravi? There was still Ravi. She had to find him. They still had people to protect, even if Blue was gone. People like Toria, as much as Petite disagreed with her methods. And Isa. If Humanity For Humans found the Resistance Base, Isa was destined for the recycling centre just like Blue.

The door clicked.

Petite rolled her head up.

Nikolai was still tall, still broad shouldered, still presented the perfect professor image with his impeccably clean lab coat and perfectly maintained hair. Petite should have known better than to trust an engineer with immaculate hands.

Instead of the smile he had first greeted her with when she had been a fresh PhD and he had been trying to recruit her, Nikolai scowled, face twisting with it.

He sat primly on the sofa opposite her and picked up a water glass. She ought to have spat in it.

"Where is it?" he asked finally.

Petite pressed her hands together and said nothing.

He rubbed a hand over his forehead, smoothing the wrinkles there. "We can do this the easy way or the hard way, Dr Palmer. Where is the data?"

"It was my work," Petite muttered.

"You agreed all the work you had would go to the project folder and when you left, it went too. Where is it?"

"It was *my* work," Petite repeated.

Nikolai surged to his feet, his face turning flush and twisting up in anger. "Where the fuck are the files! In order to delete them from the server, you must have put them on a drive. Where is it?"

"It's been years, Nikolai, you don't think it could have got lost in that time?"

Nikolai snorted. "Don't fucking play me for a fool, I know you, I know exactly what type of person you are and you would never, in a million lifetimes, misplace something that valuable. Something you designated as *dangerous* like that. So I'll ask you one more time. Where are my files?"

He was right, at least in part. Petite would never have risked letting that chip fall into the wrong hands and he wouldn't believe her even if she did tell the truth. A harsh smile broke out over Petite's face. More of a feral bearing of teeth than anything else. "Probably at the recycling centre by now."

Nikolai reared back. "You put it in that malfunctioning cyborg?"

"They were perfectly functional before you got your hands on them. I mean, come on Nikolai! Gen-3 Alpha cybes go in Gen-3 MCUs. Every half-way decent engineer knows that. But you always were a hack."

The slap shocked her more than it hurt. Her face burned with it but it didn't matter. Nothing mattered.

Nothing but getting out of here and finding Ravi.

Welcome To The End
Blue

Harsh hands dragged at Blue, jostling them like a bag of rubbish. Machine oil spread out around them, the same sparkling blue as their bands.

Their synthetic skin pieced itself back together even as their network shuddered and fizzled. Maybe it would be beyond them to recover from this. Maybe it would be better to just give up trying.

It wasn't like Blue hadn't expected Petite to have a life before she went on the run. They'd even joked about it with her, about her desire to keep it totally to herself, about Blue's similar choices to keep their past private. Blue had admired how skilled Petite was at biomechanics, at fixing up cybernetics. But Blue had never gone back to that chip full of information, except to secret it away. And now all that admiration and amusement and attraction had turned sour, swirling in Blue's mind and body like so much water trying to mix in with their oil. Fundamentally incompatible.

How could she have been the same as that asshole who had demanded Blue revert to their designation and purpose? How could she have known him? How could she have worked with a man who so clearly saw Blue as nothing different than a chair or a table?

Did she used to think like that too?

"It looks so... human." A voice filtered into Blue's consciousness.

"I know," a different voice replied. "Makes you wonder what the designers were thinking. They knew it'd have to be recycled eventually."

"No," Blue breathed. "We were designed to be repaired. Back when mech' upgrades were fixed for free."

"What?" the first voice shrieked.

Blue's face shifted into a frown even as they couldn't peel their eyes open. Was it that offensive to think that cybes might have been upgraded? Or that mech' upgrades were free too once upon a time?

"It's still alive."

"It's not human, stupid. It was never alive."

"But..." the first voice said, hesitantly, crouching by Blue in military green trousers.

Ravi had been military once, had believed in the system enough to join up. What was it about Blue that made them care for people like that? Second chances, they supposed. The eternal and endless hope that people might change their minds for the better.

"There's no way mech' upgrades could be free. How would we ever afford that kind of thing? We'd run out of supplies, out of credits."

Blue rolled their head to meet the human's eyes. "And who decides the value of credits?"

Blue closed their eyes, needing to block out at least a little of the colour rippling overstimulation. Was there any way out of this? Any way for them to avoid being carted off to a recycling centre like so many of their friends and colleagues and family all those years ago with The Crash. Just another broken cyb' to be got rid of.

Blue had never struggled with their own mortality, such as it was. Death was inevitable, every time they went on a mission they risked their immediate demise, they risked not being able to be repaired upon their return. But they had never been this close. Never been this damaged. Never been this unbearably far away from everyone they cared about.

And, as much as Blue wanted to be back with the Resistance, what they really wanted... "I should have told her."

"Told who what?"

"Petite. I should have told her every stupid day, I was just too scared she wouldn't believe me, that she would think I wasn't capable of it."

"Capable of what?"

"Love. That I love her. With my whole being. With everything I have and everything I am. Regardless of programming, regardless of who thinks I should be able, regardless of her past or mine. I love her so much it hurts to think about it too hard."

The world faded around them.

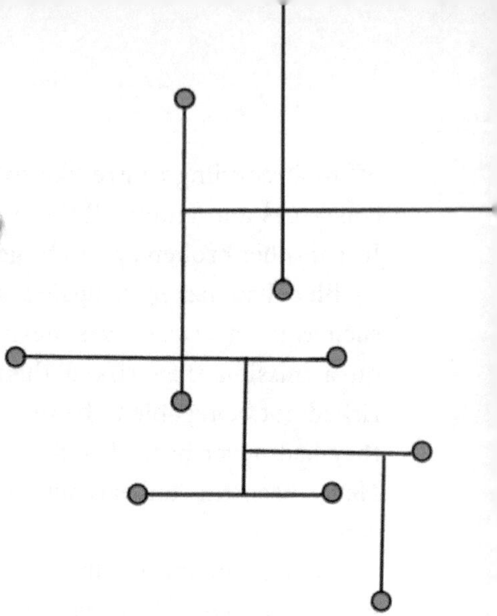

Trial

Welcome To You New Life... Again
Ravi

Ravi wanted to scream as pain flared through him. His vision blurred in the sudden bright light. He jerked upright.

Not again.

Not again not again not again.

This time, unlike the last few, more times than Ravi cared to count, no hands held him down. Nobody started talking, silence assaulted Ravi's ringing ears.

He peered around.

Petite sat on a rolley stool where the equipment cart usually was.

"P–" Ravi cut himself off before he could say more. The likelihood that they were being watched, even if Petite wasn't a double agent, and her being freely sat here upon one of his reawakenings didn't exactly reassure him that she wasn't. Either way, best to keep his recognition to himself.

"Hello Ravi," Petite said, her rough voice quiet. She gave a pointed look at the door behind him. Definitely being watched then. But still no clarity on whether Petite was trustworthy or not.

He wanted to trust her. He wanted to allow those soft, warm, firelight feelings to grow and develop and guide him. But Ravi wasn't a fool, he knew how to survive and survival didn't allow for easy trust like that, especially in the face of such a betrayal as finding out Petite used to work with the man who had been tearing Blue to pieces, that Petite was here where Ravi himself had been so poorly treated.

"You have been Re-Animated. Your memories have been suppressed by a chip in order to prevent you reliving your death."

Without thought, Ravi pressed his fingers pressed into the spot in his synthetic skin where he had stashed the memory chip.

Petite glanced at the movement, looked up at Ravi, blinked slowly as if nodding, and shot her eyes to the door behind him.

They were definitely being watched then.

And whether Petite was actually trustworthy or not, she wanted him to know that, and she knew he didn't actually have a memory chip anymore. But, apparently nobody else here knew that. "I'm confused," Ravi admitted slowly.

"That's normal, it's disconcerting to wake up and not remember any of what came before."

Ravi nodded. It had been disconcerting to wake up with absolutely no memory that first Re-Animation, and each subsequent supposed reset – for lack of a better word – was just as confusing. "I thought medical doctors were supposed to Re-Animate people."

"Yes, that's usually true, but you're a special case, Ravi.

You have brand new tech in you that nobody else has been
given yet."

"So, I'm a prototype?"

Petite nodded.

"What for?"

Welcome To The Inevitable
Petite

What For? Quite the question and one Petite certainly couldn't begin to answer here and now.

She was only here in this room with supposedly Re-Animated Ravi was because Nikolai couldn't figure something out. He'd stormed into the little interrogation room she'd been stuck in for days, the door slamming noisily against its casing. "You did something, didn't you?"

Petite blinked.

"To my pet project. You stole the research; you set us back years with that little stunt. And now you've done something else too." He huffed a breath, visibly trying to calm down enough to talk. "What did you do to the prototype?"

"What prototype?"

"He was supposed to be the perfect sleeper agent but he didn't activate. What did you do to him?"

Ravi. Ravi who has seamlessly settled into the Resistance, picked up from a mission where Petite had landed the shuttle in the wrong place. Ravi whose memory chip was supposed to be resettable and who had once upon a time been a celebrated military officer. Ravi was supposed to have betrayed them. Or possibly was meant to betray them still.

If not for people like Isa and Blue who were so welcoming, who were so willing to forgive past misdeeds for new actions and intentions, would he have clung to that previous possible self? Would he have turned naturally against them upon arrival here?

Petite snarled. "Was it you who did that crapshoot of a job of putting him back together?"

"What did you do to him?"

"I fixed him!"

"Well un-fix him!"

"You want me to make it so none of his mechanics work again?"

"I want you to fix his memory chip to work the way I wanted it to."

The way he wanted it to. The way Petite had originally attempted to build the resettable memory chip, so that engineers could pick and choose what memories to provide their Re-Ans with. Naïve, apathetic Dr Palmer hadn't asked, had just assumed, wanted to believe that those chips were to help Re-Ans remember their families without reliving their deaths. Petite wasn't so foolish.

She didn't want to do it. But it presented an opportunity. "I wouldn't be able to do anything without access."

Nikolai's frowning face reappeared as the fog on the plexi faded. "How much access?"

"Full access."

And now here she was, washed and dressed up, with as full access as she could get to Ravi and only the knowledge that they were being watched stopping her from blurting everything to him. Every single piece of information she had, including the fact that she had long ago lost the chip filled with the data she'd stolen somewhere in the Resistance base the first day she had arrived.

She'd searched for it, of course, crawled all around the kitchen area trying to find it, kept looking until her knees had been rubbed raw and her back ached and Isa had dragged her up off the floor, cleaned up her broken skin and gifted her a pair of her own trousers to replace Petite's worn out ones.

In the lab room on the station Petite had thoughtlessly assumed was a Reset Centre, she stared at Ravi.

"It's probably best we don't get into that," she answered, finally.

Ravi's eyebrows drew together but he said nothing. "Can I ask about the tech?"

"It's a new type of memory chip – all Re-Ans are fitted with memory chips to prevent them reliving their..." she trailed off. If Ravi was a traditional Re-An with his memory chip intact, reminding him of his death probably wouldn't do much. The new chip he had been given that Petite had ripped out of his head on their first meeting had malfunctioned impressively – probably due to its new, and Nikolai designed technology.

But Ravi didn't have a memory chip at all. And Petite didn't want to remind him of his death and risk him suffering under a flash memory.

"Does it prevent me from remembering my life?" Ravi asked carefully.

"That's part of what I'm here to find out. It's an active sort of chip; it should work to help us manage your memories of your Pre-An life."

Ravi's right hand, the mechanical one she had done work on formed and released a fist.

"Let me try to fix that for you," she offered, stepping up close to Ravi and peeling his synthetic skin open to see the wires inside. She'd looked before and not found the impulse controlling it, but she lived in hope. At least this way she could get close enough to whisper to Ravi.

"Blue?" Ravi asked, voice so quiet even Petite could barely hear him.

She shook her head. Blue was gone. They both had to get out of this together.

Without Blue.

She clenched her jaw against the tears that clogged her throat. There would be time enough for tears later. There would be time enough for all her feelings after they got out. Together.

"Plan?"

Petite shook her head again. She wasn't the person who made plans. She never made a plan. When she ran the first time, it had been on impulse, pieces of almost plans falling into place and falling apart around her.

Blue made plans. Toria did. Isa... But not Petite. Petite fixed things that were broken. Little, techy things, not big societal problems. She was good at those small details. She'd never been a big picture person.

"*Did* you do it? Did you fix him?" Nikolai demanded as soon as Petite emerged from the lab room, per his call.

"I did what I could," she answered honestly. She had looked properly into the mechanical side of Ravi's brain to see what other butchery Nikolai had put him under, but most of it had seemed pretty above board. But waking him up and seeing how he moved and spoke and hid his memory had been more reassuring than she could begin to put words to.

Blue might be gone but at least there was Ravi.

Petite hardly wanted to go back to the Resistance. When Blue had first been captured, Ravi and Petite had called Toria for help. She had refused to send anyone, unwilling to risk a rescue operation and demanding that Petite and Ravi return to Base with Petite's stolen knowledge.

Ravi had flicked off the radio and said, "So that's bullshit, right? We go after Blue." But now, Petite had no idea where else to go. At least with Ravi she could stomach the idea of continuing on. Otherwise she would be completely alone once again. It wasn't a life she was ready to return to, she could barely stand the thought of it. The isolation. The fear. The inability to sleep or eat or rest safely.

"What you could?" Nikolai raged. "Don't bullshit me with that, Dr Palmer. I want to know that you have made him what I intended all along."

"And what is that?" she hissed.

"A resettable Re-An."

Petite's stomach dropped out of orbit. A resettable Re-An. To do away with all the cybes – what few were left working and those in the Resistance. To throw the hexi workers already scrounging to make ends meet to the proverbial void. To use Re-Ans as what amounted to slave labour. People who had already died once, put in an infinite loop of horrible working conditions and, should anyone complain, it would count for nothing when their memory was wiped and they had to start over again.

Re-Ans were already treated as less than human. This would shove them even further down the line. What would they call them? Drones? Just like bees in a hive, designed for work like this. Especially if they picked people like Pink Drabufly, a hexi resident with no family to speak of.

The horror of it stole her breath, her words, and even her thoughts.

"Did you fix him?"

She shook her head, clinging to the desperate hope that she could still save Ravi from that fate. "I don't think that's possible. Not him. Not now."

"Then we'll just have to start with a fresh specimen. I'm sure you're not foolish enough to refuse now."

"What about Ravi?"

Nikolai waved a hand. "We can use him for something else. Sneak him back into the Resistance if he remembers where it is. Or use him as a poster boy."

"I doubt he can still fly after the attempted resets," Petite lied.

"I don't care. I'll hand him over to Major Alitin. He can do what he wants."

Error

Welcome To Suspicion
Ravi

After Petite left, Ravi half expected to be put back under, half expected to be brought oh-so-painfully back to reality to be left questioning whether his conversation with Petite had been real.

None of it provided him any clarity as to whether Petite was trustworthy. All Ravi knew was that he was meant to be a prototype for some new kind of Re-An, that he was meant to be used to break into the Resistance and take them down from the inside.

Of course, with his new memories, his Re-Animated life, Ravi could see how and why H4H hadn't been able to find the base, considering the fact that it wasn't on any of their maps or even really on their radar. No human had set foot on a planet in true memory; the stories of the planet they had fled had been lost to legend. Except the Resistance. Every single member of the Resistance had stepped feet onto actual planetary soil, and did so on a regular basis.

He remained in the lab, alone, examining the pure white walls around him and what little tools had been left in the room itself. He couldn't have said how much time passed in that endlessly bland room, not even a sign to reread over and over like he had done with the Welcome To Your New Life sign that very first day that he had met Blue and Petite.

The day Petite had flown the ship into the wrong portion of the Re-An Centre and Blue had ended up having to take the risk of entering the main body of the station and interacting with the Gen-1 cyb at the end of the hall. Looking back at that took on a whole host of potential reasoning considering Petite's revealed backstory and Ravi's apparent purpose for being Re-Animated.

Had she dropped Blue in the wrong place on purpose? Had someone slipped the Resistance false information so they would run into Ravi? Worse still, could it have been both? Petite knowing the plan was to collect Ravi and utilise him as a sleeper agent? But, if that were the case, why would she have removed his memory chip?

Ravi had nothing but questions and no real way to answer them. He didn't want Petite to be on the bigoted side of this, he wanted her relationship with Blue to have been real. He wanted his own burgeoning feelings to be something he wouldn't regret. Then again, maybe he wouldn't have the chance to regret anything if the scientists running the lab had their way. Ravi would forget everything that had made him who he was this turn around.

And wasn't it telling that he was apparently so different now, having been offered the opportunities that the Resistance could provide. And he had Blue and Petite to thank for that.

Even if Blue was apparently gone and Petite was potentially an enemy.

Ravi dropped his head into his hands, hiding his face as if blocking out the sights would make them less real. Childish, but not completely absurd.

The door swished open once again.

Major Alitin.

Ravi schooled his face, unwilling to react to the Major in any way that might reveal his prior knowledge. He couldn't get the image of the Major and pre-Crash Blue out of his head. The way they had looked at him with such fear. The way they had looked at Ravi and his unwitting memory with such distaste atop that fear. Was it fear that made people into what they were? Or was it something more palatable. Any animal could be afraid.

"Ravi," the Major greeted.

"Major," he replied.

"How did you...?"

"Uniform." Ravi gestured to the epaulets on Alitin's shoulders, at the line of decorations across his chest. They wanted him with military knowledge he wasn't sure how to use. He could play the part. He could play what he needed to survive and to get out.

Major Alitin offered a uniform, Ravi's old colonel's uniform.

Ravi swallowed thickly, dismissing those memories that had so nearly sent him into a reliving of his death that first Re-Anned day – or at least the first one he could remember. He slipped into the uniform with ease borne of decades-long habit, scraping his hair back and pulling the hat low over his eyes as he always did.

Alitin led him from the lab-style room and down a bland corridor. Ravi fell into step with him as if they were walking a parade together, even with his delayed right leg.

Ravi's own belt and pockets were empty, but the way Alitin's trousers fell betrayed the location of his multi-tool.

He reached forward to pull open a door. Over Alitin's shoulder Ravi saw a puddle of blue machine oil.

Ravi surged into motion. He grabbed Alitin's extended arm, yanked it behind his back. His free hand dipped into the pocket with Alitin's multi-tool.

He had plenty of experience exposing the blade. He pressed it against Alitin's throat. "That doctor who I woke up with." He searched his recollection for her name, the name everyone here was calling her. "Dr Palmer, where is she?"

"I don't know. That's Nikolai's prerogative."

Ravi pressed the blade tighter.

"She'll be in one of the interrogation rooms, but you can't open those doors without the right access card."

"Your access card?"

"Fuck, Simtiv, you know all military personnel are equipped with subdermal chips, what are you going to do? Carve mine out?"

He couldn't exactly drag Alitin across the station like this.

"Can't believe the fucking 'borg-lovers got inside your head. They're machines, Simtiv, not people."

"Half my body is machine, Alitin. Am I only half a person?"

"It's not the same."

"Why not?"

Alitin blustered. "It's just not."

"People are dying out there," Ravi breathed, almost desperate to be able to change Alitin's mind. "Their mech' is failing and they're dying and all we ever did was chase cyborgs. And for what?"

"We're not to question orders."

"Do you really think that's a good thing?"

Alitin shoved out of Ravi's grip, multi-tool blade nicking his throat but not badly enough to bring him down. Bright red blood trickled down his throat and into the white of his undershirt. "We're not here to *think!*"

He should have known it was pointless to argue with Major Alitin of all people. Ravi knew better than most the kind of man he was. "Then why did you always go back for that one particular cyb' at the Pleasure House?"

"What?"

"The brown eyed one. You always went for them over all the others. Why?"

"That's like having a favourite pair of shoes."

"Is it? Or was there some specific connection you formed with that particular cyb'?"

"Give me the multi-tool, Simtiv. This doesn't have to go badly for you. We'll just reset you and try again. You can go into the booth." He gestured vaguely. "Talk to the public about how great the newly improved Re-An programme is, how it let you retain or regain some of your memories, scare the fuck out of the rebellion and—"

"I'm done working against the interests of the populace," Ravi interrupted.

Major Alitin's face twisted. "Fuck, Simtiv. You always were a contrary, superior bastard." He launched himself at Ravi.

The scuffle didn't last long before Ravi's hands were warm and sticky with blood.

Alitin sunk to the ground, blood pooling around him like the machine oil that had spurred Ravi into motion.

With bloodied hands, Ravi dipped into the room with the machine oil. Blue's body had been haphazardly discarded like so much litter.

Ravi choked against tears clogging his throat. He sank to his knees beside them, hands fluttering over them, afraid his touch could cause more damage. Finally, he laid one hand against their cheek. They didn't respond.

Steeling himself, Ravi stood once again. He turned his back on the unresponsive cyb' that used to be his friend, now painted with the same kind of red handprint that stood above the others in the Resistance Base.

He pressed on down the bland corridor in a mirror of the way Blue had that first day, checking door after door.

If he could find Petite, if he could find a way off the station, if he could find a way to contact the Resistance. Toria might have threatened him should he let anything happen to Blue, but the Resistance still needed to know about the threat. Even if there was no real way Ravi expected to make it out of this station alive.

He pulled open one door to find a recording booth – the one Major Alitin had referred to? A camera hooked up to broadcasting equipment, all set up facing a chair stylised to look like a pilot's console.

At the sound of footsteps further down the corridor, Ravi slipped inside the room, jamming the door closed with the bloodied multi-tool.

He wiped his hands to the best of his ability on his blue-stained trousers and started flicking at the switches.

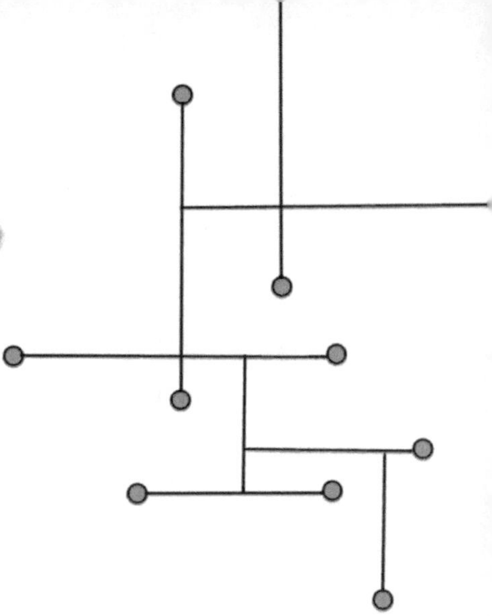

Welcome To Revolution

The scene took over all the screens on the Station, an error of unfiltered magnitude. The screens filled with a man in full, formal military uniform, Colonel's hat sat low over his face.

"My name is Ravi, but I was once known as Colonel Simtiv. I was Re-Animated, brought back to life by the military." He removed his hat and ran a hand through his hair, granting it freedom from its slicked back form, revealing his bright eyes. "For purposes they wouldn't tell me. That was months ago.

"Now, I am back in a Re-An centre, and they are pretending that this is the first time I have been Re-Animated, because they wanted to reset my memory. It didn't work. But I will not be the last attempt, if they have their way."

He glanced to the side, to a door not visible to the camera's lens then leaned forward. His eyes bored into viewers, stopping people as they walked in the streets. "They are lying to you. They are lying to us all. The Resistance are fighting for you all, regardless of background, regardless of mechanicals. We are all one accident away from needing mechanical augmentation; they will come for you next.

"I am not here to tell you what to think. I am not here to try to pitch you on cyborg rights. I am not here to let you know how mechanically augmented people are being treated. No. Instead I want to ask you a single question. This is the question that should let you decide for yourself what position you land in."

He paused, keeping the people around the screens on tenterhooks, waiting to see what this strange man wanted them to ask. "What is it that makes us human? Is it our capacity for care? The way we build communities? The way we make art? Or is it something more nebulous than even that?

"They cut you off from the people they want you to fear, specifically so that you can't see their potential for humanity. Do you really want people like that in charge?

"Do you think what they are doing is humane? Do you agree with their choices? Actively agree with them? Or is it just easier not to think too hard? Have you just been told one too many times to listen to the voice of authority?"

He swung his arms wide, one moving slower than the other, as if it didn't quite get the message. "Here I am, a Colonel, a voice of authority. And I reiterate. Ask yourself: What is it that makes us human?"

FOR NEWS ABOUT LATEST
RELEASES

Join The Mailing List At:
WillSoulsbyMcCreath.com

ABOUT THE AUTHOR

It's pronounced "Souls-Bee-Muh-Kreth"
As a cosplayer, Table-Top Gaming nerd, and videogamer;
fiction has been a staple of Will's life forever. They like to
corrupt their friends into joining these pass-times, or at
least reading their stories.
Obsessed with every way to tell a story and every possible
use for one, Will had few choices other than becoming a
writer. A little too nosy for their own good they like to
invest their time fixing other people's problems, and when
that doesn't work they hand out stories to make you feel
better.

TURN THE PAGE FOR A PREVIEW FROM
UNLICENSED DELIVERY

UNLICENSED DELIVERY
Contents Subject To Change

Matter sat in the uncomfortable chair. Supposedly chairs like this were designed to suit the maximum number of members of the Inter-Planetary Alliance; but they always wrought havoc with Matter's damaged joints. Then again, maximum tolerance didn't mean maximum comfort, and maximum tolerance was to be expected in an IPA standardised Medi-Centre, regardless of location or comfort levels.

The Harrushetti sat across from Matter blinked his slit-pupiled eyes, an icy shade of blue that perfectly matched his home planet's icy surface. A cream coloured, hand knitted jumper obscured most of his torso except for his hands, striped with the same grey and white tiger-like pattern as the hair on his head. Matter didn't like to question how it was that Harrushetti had also developed head hair or at least thicker hair on their heads than the rest of their body. Most bipedal bimanual lifeforms seemed to have, but Matter's curiosity about it was too easily overridden by their discomfort at thinking of themself having a physical form.

Or maybe it was just that they had been planet-side too long.

They shuffled in their seat.

The Harrushetti blinked again.

"Are you gonna ask me a question, or what?" Matter blurted.

The Harrushetti smiled. Something about it made Matter's hair stand on end. There was no hint of the harrushetti's sharp canines, but Matter's instincts didn't need to see them to know they were there. "I am Dr Brruuh TeaYaBin." The way his throat trilled around the 'rr' noise made Matter's brain superimpose an earth house-cat over his features. Could Matter even make a noise like that? They moved their mouth to mimic the sound silently. "I have been asked to run your cognitivilogical assessment for Deep—" he paused "—Travel."

"Did you miss a word?"

"Excuse me?"

"You paused instead of saying Space. Deep Space Travel."

Dr Brruuh TeaYaBin rolled his shoulders like he was calibrating a pounce.

Matter had studied Harrushetti behaviour – they had a Harrushetti brother-in-law after all – and a calibrating pounce movement screamed of irritation. Matter held their hands up before it went any further. "Sorry, I was just asking."

Harrushetti were known throughout the IPA for their animosity and previous warlike nature – not that any member of the Inter-Planetary Alliance was allowed to be at war, but the reputation persisted, especially thanks to the number of smaller planets within the Harrushetti galactic zone who refused to join or trade with the IPA due to their lingering resentment or even outright hostility towards Harrush itself. In all likelihood, if any of those smaller planets, galaxies, moons, or various peoples had joined the IPA first, Harrush would probably still be independent.

"I would rather you refrained." The rr's rumbled through his secondary vocal chords like a purr or possibly a growl.

"What's the difference between a purr and a growl?" Matter asked.

Dr Brruuh TeaYaBin blinked again, a little more rapidly this time.

"Like, I know a growl is a sign of aggression and a purr is pleased but acoustically, what's the difference?"

"Is where it is created. Purrs are in the chest." He touched a black clawed hand to his chest. "Growls are in the upper throat." He touched a hand to the edge of his jaw, disturbing the soft edges of his fur.

Matter's face lit up, sparkling eyes reflecting the blue undertones of the Harrushetti they faced.

Dr Brruuh TeaYaBin tilted his head. "You're Ouaeahhn?" the pronunciation was exactly as Matter would expect. More of an oo-ah-eh-ah-nn than the proper oh-Way-AAn. He looked down at his datapad, scrolling through the information. "I cannot find that in your file."

Matter shrugged, shoulders making an unpleasant pop. They really needed to get out of this chair. "Should be in there somewhere. I'm only half – it's pretty rare for people to even notice." Unless Matter got excited, or ran across another Ouaeahn. Even then, most people didn't know enough about Ouaeahn to figure it out unless they were one themself. "It's pretty well guarded info. People can get weird about it..."

"Do you want to talk about that?"

"Not particularly."

"I asked badly. No translators. Let's talk about that. It cannot be easy, hiding half of who you are."

"No translators? Really? Did you just learn a lot of languages? Or do you only work with people who already speak your languages?"

"The translators are good but they cannot cope with idioms and things akin to that. People use those a lot in cognitivism fields." Cognitivism, also known as psychology. "And it is important to understand non-verbal communication, which is not programmed into translators."

Matter knew that all too well. It was a big part of the reason they'd gone on that six week course on Harrushetti culture and communications. "That's fascinating, tell me more."

"I think it is important to have immersed yourself in a culture to understand it well enough to be able to assess—" He stopped, his eyes narrowing to slits, nose scrunching up. "I know what you are doing."

"Hmm?"

"You are trying to deflect my attention away from the task at hand."

A smile tugged at Matter's lips but they tried to contain it. "And what would that be?"

Again his nose scrunched.

Matter laughed. "Sorry, sorry. I'm just razzing you. Anoushaah."

"That is not a word I know. An-ooh-sha?"

"An-ou-SHAAAAH," Matter corrected. "It's an Ouaeahhn word – for the record, ooh-way-an or wee-un are better than the nonsense you said earlier. But Anoushaah is – it's hard to translate from Ouaeahhn, but it's like a professional apology for semi-unprofessional behaviour that was attempted in the name of fun but proved not fun for all parties involved.

"Complex."

"That's Ouaeahhn. Each syllable has a meaning. It takes forever for people to learn."

Dr Brruuh TeaYaBin blinked slowly twice.

"Is the blinking a 'thing'?"

"What?"

"It wasn't in the 'Understand a Harrushetti' data pack or the six week Culture and Communications course I took; but you keep blinking and now that I think about it Dimé does too."

"It fosters relationships. But we are not here to talk about Harrushetti relationship building."

Matter sighed. "We're here to assess my aptitude for Deep Space Travel lasting at least two years and whether I am fully aware of the dangers contained within."

"Are you going to take this professionally?"

"If you mean seriously, then absolutely not. I don't take anything seriously."

Once again Dr Brruuh TeaYaBin's nose scrunched. "I have to admit, that is not a promising position for a Deep Travel Assessment."

"No?"

"No. Deep travel is a—" he paused. "Sp-ps-pserious business." He stumbled over the s in the same way people did when they tried to coax a cat out of hiding. "Name one risk of Deep Travel and how you plan to deal with the emotional repercussions of that."

"Well..." Matter tapped a finger against their lips in an exaggerated manner. "We could all be eaten by Space

Whales!"

The cognitivist opened his mouth and paused, as if trying to mentally communicate a word before saying, "Whales do not exist."

"Whales are an Earth Ocean Mammal."

"There is no existence of ps— Galactic Whales."

"Of course there are! I've had a run in with the beasts before, they suck all the marrow out of your bones and this is why my medi-file – which is what you keep glancing at on that datapad – labels me as having an unspecified chronic condition."

Dr Brruuh TeaYaBin's voice came out flat. "You have chronic pain because a galactic whale ate your bone marrow?"

Matter put on a shocked face. "You don't believe me?"

"About any part of that tale? No. I do not believe you."

Matter grinned and shrugged. "Your problem. Look, I've done long-term and dangerous assignments before. The big risk is death – at which point, I'll be too dead to worry about it. The lesser risk is an accident that leaves me with constant pain – which I already have and am dealing with just fine. Statistically the risk is low either way and as a half-Ouaeahhn, half-Earthling I am both physically and biologically designed to cope well, especially if I have good, solid relationships with the crew – which I am guaranteed with at least one on this particular ship. You and I both know this assessment is meaningless for an experienced voyager."

Dr Brruuh TeaYaBin wrinkled his pink nose as if he wanted to growl. He scribbled something on the datapad, hands so tense his claws extended.

Maybe Matter had pushed him too far. Harrushetti

didn't take well to sudden changes of emotion; they were a steadfast people and Matter's particular brand of humour tended to set them on edge. Then again, if Dr Brruuh TeaYaBin was a quality cognitivist, he would have read Matter's file, which said they had been cleared for Deep Space Travel before. Which meant this whole assessment was entirely for the bureaucratic stamp of it having taken place. The actual content didn't matter.

Coming October 2023

ACKNOWLEDGEMENTS

Starting at the very beginning, I want to thank my mum for teaching me to read in the first place, it hasn't always been easy with my dyslexia but some of the best things never are. Thanks for all your help building this into its best version, including reminding me, once again, how many commas is too many for a single sentence.

To my In-Laws for peeking even when I told you not to, and pestering for your chance to get to read the next thing. It makes me smile every time.

To everyone who bought and read my previous books, especially those who reviewed it. I still can't believe there are people in the world who are interested in the stories I have to tell.

My friends, Stew & James, Jen, Jenny, Megan. Each of your knowledge bases and skills and humanity is a part of this novel. You are my Resistance. Thanks for standing by my side even when it feels like the world is against me.

To the writing community online, everyone who shares their writing and publishing journeys. You make me feel less alone in this endeavour.

And, as always, I save the Bexx-st for last. B, you were my inspiration for this book (in a good way), I hope it's everything you wanted it to be. Sorry I made you cry… again. I promise I'll do a happier one next time.

Thank You So Much For Picking Up A Copy of
Welcome To Humanity

For News About My Latest Releases Sign Up
To My Mailing List At:
WillSoulsbyMcCreath.com

Or come find me on Social Media, when I'm
there I'm
@nopoodles

Enjoy my FREE Short Stories over on
nopoodles.wordpress.com

www.ingramcontent.com/pod-product-compliance
Lightning Source LLC
Chambersburg PA
CBHW051221210726
48290CB00003B/741